The Cosmopolitans

Nadia Kalman

Livingston Press
The University of West Alabama

Copyright © 2010 Nadia Kalman
All rights reserved, including electronic text
ISBN 13: 978-1-60489-066-2 library binding
ISBN 13: 978-1-60489-067-9 trade paper
Library of Congress Control Number 2010929243
Printed on acid-free paper.
Printed in the United States of America,
Publishers Graphics
Hardcover binding by: Heckman Bindery
Typesetting and page layout: Joe Taylor
Cover design and layout: Lev Kalman
Cover art: Elena Kalman, Lev Kalman
Proofreading: Connie James, Joe Taylor, Tricia Taylor,
Stephen Slimp, Gerald Jones
Author's acknowledgements on page 239

F KALMAN

Livingston Press is part of The University of West Alabama
and thereby has non-profit status.
Donations are tax-deductible:
brothers and sisters, we need 'em.

first edition
6 5 4 3 2 1

The
Cosmopolitans

Куда плывете вы? Когда бы не Елена,
Что Троя вам одна, ахейские мужи?

Where are you sailing to? If Helen were not there,
What would Troy be to you, young warriors of Aegea?

— Osip Mandelstam, 1915

1

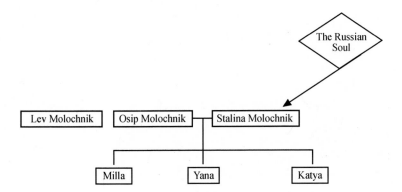

Lev

They are none of them fans of tradition. Tradition is for great-grandparents, and not even for theirs, who traded their shtetls for the Universal Struggle.

Was it traditional to leave Mother Russia, to leave it truly, not just to sit on the floor listening to an imitation folk bard sing about it? They flew to the land of the free, and they worked towards diplomas in computing, and after a few years, they could afford boom boxes to play the old wistful songs, they could afford to be tearful when they listened.

They would categorically disagree with all of the above. They would tell me I am generalizing like a Marx. They would ask, Why I don't write about Samuel: he never attended a single computer class and look at him now, a home health aide and a cocaine addict, have you ever heard of a vocation and an addiction so mismatched? Why don't I write about Pasha, who owned a wig store and was always offering us free front pieces, because *"Pochemu i net?"* why not? Who died butting her car into a highway divider, who may have died on purpose?

I say, it's no exception to think you have an exemption. Then, bowing my head, I admit that when I say all, I mean most, and when I say most, I mean my brother Osip's family, the Molochniks of Stamford, Connecticut. Nothing to do with you, Valera Stas Sasha Abram Yosha Genady Zoonia Manya Margarita Natalya Kiril Foma Galina Rachel. How could I write about you? How could I remember you, or you me?

Stamford has its North, nearer to New Canaan, home to formerly famous pro wrestlers and Gene Wilder; and its South, where we Molochniks live. However, Connecticut gives even its undistinguished residents ways to distinguish among ourselves. My brother's family lives across from a gas station, but his wife can say they live in a Tudor. I live in a low-income housing project, but I can say I live in Augustine Manor, for that is what our developer, who installed a bidet in every toilet and a coat of arms below the "No Solicitation" sign, chose to call it.

I've climbed to the roof, free from my neighbors' footfalls, their warring cooking smells, ignoring my knees and the No Trespassing sign, for one reason only: to scratch out a pleasant, simple tune.

Nadia Kalman

Milla

"That's not how it starts, you know," one of the uncles said. There were three uncles at the table: a doctor, an editor-Quaker, a novelty tee shirt maker; all tall, all dark, all maybe-handsome if they weren't so old, in their forties, maybe. Milla was twenty-one, at a Seder with her boyfriend Malcolm Strauss's family, in a Manhattan apartment on the park, with unwashed hair (it had been a last-minute invitation), her lip balm under one leg, her leg under Malcolm's hand, pecking with her spoon at a matzo ball and guessing at etiquettes, a large and poorly concealed pimple on her chin.

"No one in America knows how *Anna Karenina* really starts," the uncle went on.

"What?" Malcolm's mother Jean said, her hands at her throat. She'd wanted to be a musical-theater actress, but was a divorce lawyer instead.

"Everyone in the English-speaking world just quotes it like that. The original translation was incorrect, but it was a tremendous hit, so they just kept it." Milla was now fairly sure it was the doctor uncle. He was the most confident one, according to Malcolm. Everyone had always thought he would win the Nobel Prize, and even though he hadn't, even though the tee shirt maker was wealthier, and the editor-Quaker more cultured, the doctor remained the grandmother's favorite.

"So how does it really start, then?" Jean said. "Milla, you must know."

Eight? Twelve? Sixty? beautifully groomed heads turned towards her. Malcolm squeezed her leg. "Actually, I think it does start: 'Happy families are all alike,' just like in the translation," she said.

"But Richard just said it doesn't," Jean said.

"Yes, but Russian people are very educated," said one of the aunts. She was now Milla's favorite. Milla would remember her by her, well, her fatness, which just made her all the more beautiful and maternal. "Pasha, for instance," the aunt continued. "Our 'housekeeper'?" She made scare quotes around the word with her fingers and a few Strausses smiled. "In Russia, she was a dentist."

"Huh." Jean said. "Malcolm, do you know?"

"About what?"

"The first line of the book, aren't you listening?"

Malcolm smiled, leaned back in his chair. "I'm just a music major."

"What do you *do* with a music major?" Jean asked the group. She pointed at Malcolm like a cop about to shoot and he pointed back at her and Jean smiled, letting him off for now.

Looking around the table, Uncle Doctor said, "*Anna Karenina* starts with the couple arguing, and *then* Tolstoy puts that line, as an explanation. I read about it in the *New Yorker*, I'm pretty sure, so…" He gave a modest shrug.

"When I last reread *Anna Karenina* —" Milla made sure to pronounce the title with a Russian accent — "it started with 'Happy families.'"

"And you read the book in the Russian? The whole thing?" Jean said.

"Of course," Milla said, trying to imitate the tone of Jean's voice when, earlier in the evening, she'd told the family about a peerless eye cream. "I'm positive I'm right." She waved her spoon like a sickle.

"Hmm," Malcolm's mother said. "Bobby? Do you agree?"

Bobby was Malcolm's father. Chubby as a seal, he wore a black suit with lavender stripes, which Jean had bought for him, and had said nothing for the entire meal, except to agree with Jean that the suit was, indeed, incredible. "Never read it," he said now.

"But you went to Harvard!" Jean said. "*And* he's never seen *The Philadelphia Story*."

The aunt who, throughout the dinner, and apparently, throughout the past three months, had been exhorting them to party as if it were 1999, said, "Send him to the lions."

Malcolm smiled and said, "I never saw it either. I don't like that actress."

"You don't like Katharine Hepburn?" Jean's face now carried an expression of stupefaction so extreme her eyes had crossed.

"She's too hard, and I don't like her voice, and she's not sexy." He was so easy here, everywhere. He slurped a spoon of soup.

"I know your problem," Jean said.

"What's that?" As he slung his arm around Milla's shoulders, she thought of how well she slept, with his arm just like that, and let her chest relax into the thought of him.

Jean said, "You just don't like strong women."

"Yeah, I do. Milla's strong." He paused. "Still waters run deep."

Attempting to prove she was loud, boisterous, even, Milla ventured, "You know, in Russia, there's this saying, *v teehom omute cherti vodyatsah*, devils live in quiet waters. So, you never know." Silence. Deep-set Straussian eyes stared from all directions.

"Great *broth*," the uncle who made tee shirts finally said.

Osip

Everything was in confusion in the house of the Molochniks. The Chaikins were due to arrive in an hour, along with their son, Leonid, a stock analyst with a face like a potato, who'd bought himself two mountain bikes, just in case the right girl came along. That girl, according to Osip's wife, was Milla, but Milla drooped through the house, a dying swan in sweatpants. She'd mentioned the Chaikins' visit to her boyfriend Malcolm, and Malcolm had said that if she was seeing other people, he would, too. Osip thought his beautiful Milla had nothing to worry about — Malcolm was not a James Bond — but who cared what Osip thought? No one even cared that he was wearing the fuzzy checkered sweater his wife had put in the trash the previous week.

Yana, their middle daughter, tried to work the word "clitorectomy" into every conversation, as if it were the name of a boy she loved, and had created a mountain of what she called "girl clothes" in the upstairs hallway, and the mountain was slowly collapsing, skirts fluttering to the floor whenever anyone passed, and she was taking photographs of this.

Katya, the youngest, had locked herself in the bathroom again. Was she dyeing her hair? Cutting off her eyelashes like she had that one time? Smoking crack, like the police chief's daughter on *The Commish*? Creating a viable hydrogen fuel?

Osip stood at the table and watched his wife whip meringues. "*It's perfect,*" she said in her meticulously Muscovite Russian. "*Milla's an accounting major, and accounting is a little lower than stock analyzing. So the woman is a little lower than the man, and the man feels good, and they talk about business.*" Every few seconds, she wiped the counter clean of batter, only to splatter it again, only to wipe it again. This was completely contradictory to the Just-In-Time manufacturing techniques Osip had just learned at work, which he could resist sharing with her only because he had a more important

Nadia Kalman

mission.

"*God loves the trinity*," everyone had said when Katya was born. Osip loved the trinity too, but he had always wanted a son, for the sake of one important Jewish word: moderation. Many of the Molochniks' problems stemmed from the immoderate number of girls in the house. A boy would tell Yana that Osip wasn't actually very patriarchal at all. A boy would address Katya in the street language of modern youth: "Tell me the dealio with all those earrings, and failing math, when you have a father to tutor you, yo," and she would explain herself, and then Osip would know what to do. It wasn't natural, him alone, battling all these forces.

Stalina called up the stairs, "*Yanka — are you waiting for Pushkin to set the table? Get to it, girlie.*"

Yana said, "Why? So the prospective owner of Milla's vagina can think she's tidy?" and clattered down in her steel-toed boots.

"You give me headache already," Stalina said. Whenever anyone spoke English to her, she took it as a dare.

"Shh, little girl, shh," Yana said, "Your voice will never be privileged." She began tossing silverware onto the table.

"Katya," Stalina called up the stairs. "*Nu*, come on."

The Commish, Osip's favorite television policeman, off the air four years now, but never to be forgotten, would say now or never, junior. "*You know that program at the Jewish Community Center, 'Tolerance Now'?*"

"No," Stalina said, chopping an apple into a variety of abstract shapes.

Osip deployed Zionism. "*It's to benefit Israel. They send children to Jerusalem, and bring other children here.*"

"*Children should stay where their parents put them.*" She looked up from the apple battlefield. "*These other children, who are they?*"

"*They're Muslims, Stalinatchka, but from nice countries, Bangladesh, Egypt, these are the ones who, if they see someone making a bomb, they can say something like, 'Look here, my fellow Allah-enjoyer, I've lived with a few Jews myself, and they're really not so bad.'*" Stalina raised her flour-hoary eyebrows. "*He'll say, 'Did you know Jews invented the hologram?' Because we'll have taught him things like that, veedish, see?*"

"What is the Point of Stamford?" Stalina said. Osip knew what was coming: a speech she often gave to visiting Boston friends. *"It's provincial, yes, without question. However: have you noticed, historically, that most blockades and suchlike happen only to large, important cities? No one cares about Stamford, so it's safe."*

He grabbed her shoulder. *"And that's exactly —"*

"But when you start bringing devils to these quiet waters —"

"Devils? Stalinatchka!" he said, possibly overplaying his shock. *"People used to call us that."*

Yana came back in and took some glasses from the cabinet. Stalina asked about Katya; apparently, she remained in the bathroom.

"Still? And Milla?" Stalina said.

"The hozaika vlagalishta, keeper of the vagina, is in my room."

Stalina said, *"When you're done, tell Milla to get down here. And get Katya out of the bathroom — Milla needs to make herself up. And enough with trying to shock us with your feminist tricks. That's not even the word Russian people use — they say pipka, for children, or zhenskiy organ, which is more polite, or pizda, to be crude, right, Osya? You think you can shock me?"* Stalina lifted a ladle of meringue batter. *"When you and your sisters had full diapers, guess who had to clean your pipkas?"*

Yana clattered back upstairs, muttering something about Stalina being a rebel.

Osip said, *"The boy the JCC has for us is a graduate student, in industrial engineering. Maybe Katya will let him tutor her in math."*

"Katya doesn't need a tutor, she needs to listen to her mother and learn some manners. Like you, why are you just standing there like a prince? Finish the salad."

"Of course, zaychik."

"And don't call me zaychik. I'm a big fat woman, not a little bunny rabbit."

Quick as a fox, he got three cucumbers, a bag of spinach, and four tomatoes from the refrigerator, laid them on the counter as a symbol of good faith, and wrapped his arms around his wife's waist. *"You, big and fat? I can put my hands around you, practically."*

"What's this 'practically' supposed to mean?"

"It means you're tiny, all bones, come kiss me, my little bone-

bag." Osip's kiss scattered the flour, exposing purple rouge. "*And you know, it doesn't look like Lev's ever moving into that extra room, he lives the bachelor life now.*"

"*What life?*" Stalina was beginning her Lev lecture. It was time for Osip to deploy his most powerful weapon.

"*Do you know, there are no Russian host families on the list right now? We don't want those JCC people to think only Americans can be generous.*" He paused to let it sink in. "*They'll say, those Russians just come to take our charity, never give anything back.*"

A tornado rose in the mixing bowl. "*The terroristnik will be your responsibility, understand?*"

"*Yes, zaychik, let me kiss your pink nose...*" Osip was saying, when Milla slouched into the room. Osip tried to smile at her, but she didn't notice.

Stalina said, "*Sit down, Millatchka. What are all these tears? Osya, what are you doing? We have forty-five minutes exactly. Will you be able to find it within yourself to cut a cucumber before then?*"

Eyes on the floor, Milla said, "You know what's wrong."

"What, Malcolm? But Milla, *bood' milloi*, be kind, like your name, like your mama is asking, Chaikins will be here in forty-four minutes, what you want for them to do? Cry with you for boy you've known a few months?"

"Seven months."

"Seven months."

"You're right, seven months, who cares? Let's party."

Osip tried to hand Milla a new tissue, but she seemed to be reading a secret message on her sweatpants.

"I don't know why you get ironical," Stalina said. "Leonid is stock analyst." She put down her whisk: what more was there to say?

Milla said, "I just want to be with Malcolm. I don't know why you forced me into this setup."

"Ah, and I force you also to tell Malcolm?" Milla rolled the tissue between her hands until it resembled a cigarette.

"*Milla, bood' milloi, listen to me,*" Stalina said in a softer voice, and in Russian. "*You don't want to be an old maid like I was, until I met your father, everyone laughing about you, the husbands of your* colleagues thinking they can kiss you. You're in college; it's the right time to meet the right man."

"Malcolm was the right man."

"If Malcolm were the right man, he would hear about Leonid and hustle down here and propose. But no. Malcolm is the kind of man who will maybe marry someone when he's forty and she's pregnant."

"You don't know, you only met him like once."

"And where did you first meet him? In the park, like pigeons. He should be studying and not running to the park. Milla. Did you ever put on a miniskirt, like I told you to, and sit outside the hospital?"

"Malcolm goes to Yale!"

"And he'll keep going until he's thirty. Those professors can tell he's nerazviti, underdeveloped."

Stalina flogged her topic. Osip tried to make the radishes into stars, as his grandmother Baba Rufa had done, and dropped new tissues into Milla's lap.

"Now is time," Stalina finally said, her English taking the place of a concession, "for you to go upstairs and put on something coquetlivaya. See how I am?" Stalina passed her tiny raccoon hands over her low-cut brown blouse. "And heels high. See how long my legs are looking? If you just try a little bit, you can look like the painting Neznakomka. You have nice cheeks and black hair like Strange Lady in painting, but she has the style. She has little hat, yes, Osya?"

In the end, Milla agreed to wash her face and change her clothes. Stalina tried for mascara, was rebuffed, took it in sportsmanlike fashion. Milla had reached the kitchen door before Osip could muster a properly hearty, "No more crying, or I'll give you something to really cry about."

Milla

Upstairs, Yana sat atop a pile of clothing she planned to donate to less enlightened women, bracing herself on one foot while taking photographs of the other. Whereas Milla, trying to save their parents money, had insisted that state college would be fine, Yana had fought and won herself Columbia, professors who interested themselves in her feet.

Milla kicked desultorily at the pile until Yana looked up from the camera. "Apparently, a skirt is the least I can do," Milla said. She sat on the rug. It was the closest thing to her and she was too tired to stand. "Is there something here that would fit me?"

Yana raised an eyebrow. Actually, she raised both. She'd been practicing for years, but still hadn't mastered it. "You're just letting her pimp you out?"

"Yes. I am just letting her pimp me out." Milla sighed, traced a woolen flower with her finger. Yana seemed to want a debate. "I can't wear my own clothes, okay? Everything I own, except for these, I wore with Malcolm, so I can't wear it."

Yana half-rolled off the pile, a bubble skirt tumbling in her wake, and sat herself next to Milla. "I know. In the middle of dinner, you could drop a tampon. That always freaks guys out," she said, with the hard-bitten authority of one who'd done accidentally what she was proposing Milla do on purpose.

Milla shook her head.

"Come on. You know Mom would be all…" They looked at each other. It was impossible to imagine what their mother would be like. Milla waited for another unhelpful idea to alight upon her sister. There was something restful about watching this process cycle through. "Hey," Yana said, hitting her on the arm, "Now that you and Malcolm are taking a little break, don't worry, you'll totally get back together, but now, you get a chance to explore your sexuality."

Milla nodded and tried to believe the part about getting back together.

"You could find out you like women, or peeing on people." Yana crawled forward and pulled a plaid skirt, a black sweater, and heels from the pile.

"What's wrong with the sweater?" Milla said.

"Too low-cut. It's all, 'Come taste my melons, honeybees.'" Yana pointed her index fingers at her flat chest.

Milla stepped out of her sweatpants and reached for the skirt. Although Yana's break would go on for another week, Milla's ended tomorrow. She would have to wake up at six, drive the road that for seven months had meant returning to Malcolm. Now, it would only mean returning to her eight o'clock auditing class. It would feel like a road through the shadow of the valley of death, where Jesus was supposed to be with you so you did not fear, but, being Jewish, Milla would be alone. Would this breakup drive her to Christianity? She should tell Malcolm: he, whose parents were such big Jews, was responsible for assimilation. A tear, on behalf of the Jewish people, came to her eye.

Yana put an arm around her and led her to the large mirror in their parents' room. They looked together into the frame. The skirt was longer on her than it had been on Yana. Milla had been shocked by sadness into looking like she was fourteen, a Catholic-school girl, of the actual, not music-video, variety. Could sadness make your ankles thicker? She could tell that Yana, inexperienced in having something nice to say, was furiously attempting to summon a compliment. She cried again, for Yana's underdeveloped social skills.

Katya

Katya was neither dyeing her hair nor shaving it off. She was taking neither drugs nor a pregnancy test. She was not, in short, doing any of the things her parents feared.

Katya was trying to feel happy, while simultaneously preventing the voice of former Soviet premier Leonid Brezhnev from coming out of her mouth.

The bathroom, in which her mother had installed light bulbs too bright for the sockets, light bulbs that fizzled in complaint and burned the backs of your eyes, was not the best place for Katya's work, but she had no lock on her bedroom door and both her sisters were home.

She turned to the shower curtain, which had a map of the U.S. (purchased by her father: no one taught geography in American schools) and put her finger on New York, squeezed her eyes shut, tried to ignore the pear-shaped light-ghosts. Happiness...New York...She was Sid Vicious's girlfriend (Yeah, she knew he was dead, punk was dead, so what), not one he'd want to kill, like Nancy Spungeon, but a good one, one who'd smear oil on his face to make the pimples come, who'd chase away the MTV magnates with an axe. "I'm punk enough for the both of us," she imagined herself saying to a sniveling Sid. She was on stage, screaming out:

> Fuck — memory!
> Fuck — society!
> Fuck — the words you say!
> Fuck — come what may!

She was particularly proud of the change in meaning between the third and fourth *fuck*s.

The crowd moshed, screaming her name. Not her regular name, Katya, but her punk name, *Vonyuchinka*, which meant "the stinking one" in Russian. She opened her mouth to vomit down on them — "*Comrades, thanks to your most efficacious efforts, gross radish production has risen by an unheard-of and heroic percentage of six and three tenths...*" Could her sisters hear her out in the hallway? They — or, rather, Yana — continued to talk.

She waited for it to wind down, smothering her mouth with a leopard-spotted towel.

"It's time to go downstairs," Yana said through the door. "Are you on your cell phone?" Brezhnev grunted something about ironworks. "Are you too cool to answer?"

"Or — not cool enough," Milla said, with a smile in her voice. Katya, still lip-locked to her towel, felt proud to be cheering her sister up after her breakup. It was great to be such a loser that, just by locking yourself in a bathroom, you created a party everywhere else.

Yana said, "Time to face Potatoface."

Milla didn't laugh. Ha. Yana always thought she was so funny.

Katya lifted her face from the clammy towel, watched in the mirror as her lips finally stilled.

The first time had been at her fourth birthday party. As she unwrapped a gigantic stuffed monkey, a man's voice burst from her chest, saying something about disobedience in Romania, and her mother scooped her up and carried her to the bathroom, sat on the edge of the tub and said, "*Moy Greh,*" and cried.

Katya had thought *Greh* meant *Greek*, and kicked a Greek girl in her day care center for weeks afterwards. Finally, she summoned up the courage to check the word with Milla. It turned out that it meant sin. Milla had been nice about it; nice, but nosy. Katya had pulled her furry hood over her face and stuffed her mouth with the salty hairs until Milla stopped asking.

Years later, during one of her parents' parties, she realized whose voice it was. Everyone was drunk and trading impressions. "*Systema-titty,*" her mother's friend Edward had growled, in an unmistakable tone, and everyone instantly guessed: Brezhnev, the unwitting erotic wordsmith, "Our Nabokov."

She bit her lip to stop remembering and took out her flask. Vodka made Katya feel very cultural, very right. It allowed her to go to school sometimes, to answer questions sometimes. It was, as she'd learned in ninth grade health class, a "powerful depressant."

Milla

Katya had escaped upstairs, and Yana had invented some task in the kitchen, of all places for her to be. Roman, the new-immigrant nephew the Chaikins had living with them, had been shooed by Alla Chaikin to the den to practice his English in front of the television.

The Chaikins had already complimented Stalina's newest Art Deco statuette, of an Asian man in mid-twirl, hand cocked at his side, a whip in his fist. They had enquired about her uncle Lev, who still hadn't left his apartment, which was crazy; and about her grandmother Byata, who'd moved to Boston, which was equally crazy. All the parents had agreed America would be well-rid of Hillary Clinton, a woman utterly lacking in *zhenstvinost*, feminine charm, as well as any genuine feeling for Israel. Having concluded those preliminaries to their mutual satisfaction, the parents now freely bestowed their energies upon Milla and Leonid.

Alla Chaikin said to Milla, "*Leonid sounds like the name of an old commissioner, or Leonid Ilyich Brezhnev, even.*" She shuddered at the thought. "*Lenya's eyebrows look nothing like Brezhnev's. Call him Len-Len, like you did in Rome.*"

Arkady Chaikin said, "*Yes, and she chased him around. 'Len-Len, I have such a good prince-and-princess book for you.'*"

"*But he'd say, 'Father, hide me!'*" said Alla Chaikin. "*He didn't like books.*"

"*He still doesn't,*" said Arkady Chaikin.

"*Such an American,*" said Alla Chaikin.

Leonid Chaikin modestly lowered his gaze.

"*He doesn't have time to read,*" Milla's mother said. "*Didn't he just get promoted?*"

"*Who told you?*" Mrs. Chaikin said, and then, quickly, "*And do you know the first thing he bought with his raise?*"

"Ma," Leonid said. He hooked his thumb in his suspenders. Only he and the Brooks Brothers mannequin in the mall ever wore suspenders.

"*Tell us,*" Stalina said, putting a playful hand over Leonid's mouth. His face looked especially large compared to the hand. Milla couldn't believe that her mother was willingly touching his lips.

"*I'm not bragging,*" Mrs. Chaikin said, and Stalina vigorously shook her head. "*It's just very interesting, because Arkady and I, we never even knew things like this existed. Show them, Lenka.*"

Leonid removed Stalina's hand. "Come on, Ma."

"You are come on," Mrs. Chaikin said.

"*Batyushka, my lord,*" Stalina said. "*Millatchka, look.*"

Milla lowered her eyes to the object in Leonid's hand: a gold money clip. They were all so *gauche.* How could her mother, who had taught her that word, betray her own standards so completely? She wished she could tell Malcolm how awful they all were, but she would never have that chance again.

"It's just more convenient than a wallet," Leonid said. "When I went to Japan, they —"

Stalina said, "No apologies, Leonchik. You saw something perfect, and you grabbed." She rolled this last sentence in Milla's direction as if it were a tank.

Roman

Roman's mother wasn't always a *narcomanka*, but she was always a hairdresser, which was bad enough, a girl from a good Jewish family. To their credit, all their relatives had made dire predictions about his mother for years, which mitigated Roman's surprise when, at age eight, he had returned from a field trip to the Institute of Metal Testing to find his mother asleep on the couch, shiny-skinned, a needle sticking out of her arm like a helpful arrow in a diagram.

A few years ago, his mother had found Love! with a man who sold underwear on the street and claimed a Mafia connection. That was what she'd been looking for all along, didn't Roman understand? He'd get there soon enough himself.

The more this new love beat her, the more heroin she needed, and the more heroin he provided, the more he beat her. One night, Roman jumped on the man's back, and his mother took out one of the kitchen knives. Its ultimate destination was to be Roman. He finally agreed to go stay with his aunt and uncle in America.

Now, Roman sat alone in the Molochniks' den, watching the same program he had watched in Russia: beautiful American teenagers lit another beach bonfire. During the commercials, he redrew X's on the backs of his hands. Someone had left half a beer on the coffee table. He reminded himself he was straight-edge now.

A girl came in, darkening the room with her black-hole hair.

"You can change," he said, holding out the remote control. She must be one of the Molochnik daughters. His aunt had told him they were *intelligentniye* girls, so he'd thought they would be ugly. This girl changed the channel to one on which some boys were flopping their hair around and breaking mirrors. The music was all right, a little soft for him. He preferred hip-hop and rap.

"MTV?" he said.

"MTV sucks." With jerky little motions, she sat on the floor. She was a scrawny mosquito, but sexy, but probably a druggie, but a rich *Americanka*, so she'd be okay. Not that drugs were okay for anyone, he let the X's remind him.

"You go to high?" That was wrong, he could tell from her expression. He couldn't grind away at English any more. *"Do you go to university?"*

"In school," she said, in a laughably heavy American accent.

"Do you like this band?" Now the main boy was drawing a piece of mirrored glass across his throat, but no blood came out.

"They're a little soft," she said.

"I think the same!" He told himself to calm down and furrowed his brow, which people said made him look older. *"But seriously, they are —* posers."

She turned and smiled, only on one side of her mouth, a little suspicious. Her teeth were fine. If she only used a few drugs, it was okay, he'd teach her the straight-edge lifestyle.

"So, do you have a young friend?" he said. She squinted. Her nose also squinted. "Boo? Mac?" He gave secret thanks to MTV: Russia.

She shook her head, and behind her, a man stretched a stick of gum across a city street.

"Really?" Could he pull this off? Only in Russian. *"It's just that you're so* cool *and* hot."

Her face turned red, and she said in a familiar male voice, no American accent at all: *"The Israeli aggressor has finally revealed its predatory —"*

And his face was set to laugh, because it was a joke, wasn't it? She hopped up, still speaking — *"Never before has an invader —"* and slammed the door shut.

Leonid

Leonid, upon being tipsily instructed by his mother to run off and play with Milla Molochnik, found himself on an allergy-inducing carpet opposite an implacable foe. Meanwhile, his cousin Roman was probably jacking off in the TV room. That option was not open to Leonid, no, he had to be a model of excellence for all Russian boys in the tri-state area, had been ever since, and even slightly before (thanks to his SAT scores), his acceptance to Harvard seven years ago.

He wasn't interested in this Brezhnev-browed lump, who jerked like an epileptic every time the phone rang, displacing the Scrabble tiles; didn't she know he could be banging a hot model right now? Or at least his group's cute-from-behind secretary, in a few years, when he'd risen a bit more in the hierarchy, gotten his MBA? Didn't this Milla know this was his only night off for the next five weeks? Still, he roused himself to say, "So, do you ski downhill? Ever get out to Aspen?" Most Russians only knew how to ski cross-country, only knew small hills, slow speeds. Perhaps she was different; he was open to that possibility.

She shrugged with one shoulder. At least she was quiet. From the dining room came the voice of Yana, the hairy middle sister. "That *is* racist."

Leonid's mother said, "*No, Yanatchka, I like the black people very much. I've often wished I could be merry like a black lady.*"

Yana stomped past them and upstairs, slammed a door, and then must have turned on some rap music.

Leonid said, "Do you like rap? Snoop Dogg?"

"Snoop Dogg is for rapists." Milla's mouth twisted strangely during this sentence, as if she were in a language class. Had he heard her correctly? He'd known her since they were little, but she was acting very differently tonight. Perhaps she had developed a crush on him, and was trying to flirt, by arguing? His mother had told him that her mother had some romantic ambitions for the two of them. He turned partly away so as not to meet her glare, or stare, or whatever she thought she was doing.

From the kitchen issued some strange Russian words being, in a manner, sung. He couldn't understand all the words — some kind of animal, maybe a goat, or was it a nobleman, marching, banging on a drum, and the drum was made out of the goat's or nobleman's skin. Neither definition made complete sense for both the marching and the drum-skin. This kind of thing was exactly why he'd never taken any poetry at Harvard.

Next, he heard some ostentatious clapping, and Mrs. Molochnik saying, "*All right, Osya. Don't beat the table, it didn't do anything to you.*"

Mr. Molochnik said, "*Think, my friends, how our bards sacrificed. Alexander Galich: imprisoned, murdered.*"

"*I think he was only exiled,*" Leonid's father said.

"*He died trying to fix a radio, right, Arkady?*" Alla said.

"*You don't think the KGB had its dirty tentacles all over that transistor? You are like children.*"

"Osya," Mrs. Molochnik said.

"*Forgive me, what do I know? What's the point of arguing? He's dead, dead, dead all the same.*"

Mrs. Molochnik said, "*Osip Mikhailovich, what do you say about getting a little sleep?*"

"*I understand,*" Mr. Molochnik said. "*This is a time to talk about happy things. Bim bom, bim bom, that's what we should be singing.*" He shuffled past Leonid and Milla, raising a hand in greeting or farewell, and made his way up the stairs, still bim-boming.

"Your turn," Milla said. Leonid put down the word *Zen*, which, breathing noisily through her nose, she challenged and disqualified. He only had to play one turn after that — a meek *tree* — before his parents collected him.

Nadia Kalman

Milla

Back in her room, back in her sweatpants, Milla called her grandmother.

"*Da, lyagushinka, little frog, what's the matter?*" Baba Byata said. She had nicknamed Milla, her favorite granddaughter, "little frog" on account of her long tongue, with which Milla was able to touch her nose. Her grandmother's delight in this nickname, and in demonstrations of its origins, was a small, guilty reason that Milla had been a little bit relieved when she'd moved to Boston.

Milla told her grandmother everything and a bit more. She called Leonid Chaikin a capitalist pig and her grandmother said, "*Da, I understand,*" with only a slight bit of irony: she still believed in the ideals of Communism and the treacheries of money-lust.

"*I showed him,*" Milla said, and told a slightly exaggerated version of her Scrabble victory, which confused her grandmother, who had never played, and Milla had to explain about the values of letters, and it wasn't as satisfying to tell this part of her story as she'd anticipated. She said, "*Still, it's very sad, to have your parents stand in the way of your true love.*"

"*Da, da.*"

"*I wish you were right here,*" Milla said. Her grandmother was wearing, she knew, a polyester housecoat with cheerful, to Byata's way of thinking, green flowers with orange stems. The housecoat was buttoned to the neck and scratched Milla's forehead, not unpleasantly, all those times she'd cried into it. She invited her grandmother to Stamford.

Byata said, "*It's such a long trip, the train stinks...*"

"*But I'd cook for you. I just learned to make chicken a l'orange. That's a French chicken recipe. Mom would be happy, too, she keeps talking about taking you shopping for supplements.*"

"*Yes, your mother's very,*" Byata took a breath, "*activnaya.*"

"*So,*" Milla said, hoping that her grandmother might, in sympathy for Milla's plight, answer her question honestly, *"did you move to Boston to get away from Mom? I would understand, totally."* She began to tell again about what Stalina had said about Malcolm, and how Stalina had probably set out to ruin their love, because she was jealous.

"You know, lyagushinka, in these modern times, you can just call that boy you like."

A few minutes later, Milla took a deep breath and dialed the number she'd been trying to forget. "Am I interrupting?" She imagined a pyramid of beautiful girls in underpants, standing on one another's shoulders to make the shape of a "Y," for Yale, and for the questions of "why" he had ever bothered with someone like her, before tumbling down onto his bed.

Malcolm said no, he'd just come through the door. He'd been working on his thesis, listening to this amazing vocalist, Ori Shacktar, she'd been in the Israeli army, klezmer could be really raw, did Milla know that?

Milla told him about how rude she'd been to Leonid. "You dumped me, and he hates me, and now I have to marry him."

"I — what?"

"You don't understand my culture!" She sounded like Yana.

"Hey, hey, calm down. You always take what I say the wrong way."

Milla tried to take the deep breaths — five counts in, five counts out — her father had taught her in her crybaby youth. She said, "I hardly ever cry, you know that."

"Anyway, you don't want to marry that other guy, you want to marry me."

"I never said that, what makes you say that?"

"I want to marry you, okay? I think it would be fun to be married to you. I mean, this isn't a proposal, I'm only twenty-three, it's more — a proclamation. Yeah, a proclamation. Of love."

Milla thought to look at herself in the mirror. It was her there, not a raw klezmer singer, not a model, but her own face, crazed with happiness.

Nadia Kalman

Yana

*Since I drank of the cup of love,
I shall love forever secretly.*

"The roots of the modern-day 'love discourse' first appeared in medieval France, where troubadours such as Raimbaut d'Aurenga (cited above) found that both common and noble audiences preferred songs of heterosexual" — what? Strivings? Yana rose and strode about the room. She'd use her old favorite: "*limning* heterosexuality, and so decided to 'produce' these ballads in large quantities. Commercial considerations, then, have always been behind the perpetuation of the idea of romantic love."

Yana sat back and looked at her paragraph. Was that a Marxist-feminist critique, or what? Her professor edited a journal of advanced studies. She imagined whispers following her across campus, "only undergraduate ever to publish..."

Or, was she being "tendentious, sophistic and repetitive" again? That was what the professor had written, in small, embarrassed letters, on the back of her last paper. She wished her parents could help her, that she had the kind of parents who'd been doled out to so many of her college classmates (although not to the few who'd agreed to be her friends), parents who read and debated their children's papers over Thai, and contributed to progressive judges' re-election campaigns, and paid psychiatrists to help their children figure out where their parenting had failed. Yana would have settled for parents who didn't either laugh (Stalina) or become enraged (Osip) that she was trying to write like a Marxist. Instead, she was on her own, basically, and she had yet to answer the question: Why did audiences keep asking for love songs?

Milla bounced into the room, apparently in the manic stage of the bipolar disorder she'd acquired upon meeting Malcolm. "He's going to marry me!"

So he's going to do the honor of making you his domestic slave? So he's generously agreed to depress you, to load you up with stress- and childbirth-related illnesses, to ensure you die approximately five years earlier? Milla waited, frozen into her smile. Yana imitated the freshman girls who'd stopped to eat the chocolate and caramel cookies at the Women's Center table at orientation, before they'd realized what the cookies represented, but after Yana had begun telling them about an upcoming all-woman dance. "Uh-huh?" she said, and she probably gave the same pained smile the freshman girls had.

"It wasn't a formal proposal, that'll be later." Milla found, almost with relief, several worries: sure, Malcolm wanted to marry her now, but what if something happened between now and the engagement? Had Yana ever heard of promise rings? Did she think Malcolm had heard of them? If he had, and wasn't planning on buying Milla one, wasn't that weird? Was that weird, or was she being too demanding?

Yana said, "You know, marriage as the fulfillment of romantic love is a nineteenth-century construct."

Milla wound a curl around her finger. "That can't be true."

Yana found evidence on the Internet, but Milla just kept asking the same questions over and over again, until Yana surrendered. "You look good in white."

Worrying about whether she'd be able to get to sleep, Milla returned to her room, and Yana opened her book to a lyric by Arnaut Daniel:

> And when I see her blond hair,
> her body lean and fresh
> I love her more than I love one
> who'd give me Luzerne.

A skinny blonde. Of course. Not that it was necessarily easy to be the ideal. Yana was sure it was difficult, sometimes. She had read about it.

She typed, "Troubadours put women on pedestals, where they stood in their restrictive skirts: lifeless statues, not equal partners. In idealizing their love objects, troubadours murdered them, basically."

Yana began to pace again. Katya wasn't back yet. How could their parents possibly believe she was still at the library at ten on a Sunday night? If the last few evenings were any indication, Katya would return at two, tumbling out of a car that barely stopped. She might be laughing, for a few seconds at least, slipping across the icy lawn, before making her way inside. Yana told herself again that it was all right to tell their parents about Katya's lies, promised herself to tell them tomorrow, knew she wouldn't.

Osip

Osip awoke from dreams of frying potatoes with the great bard Galich. Stalina was hunched up with her rear in the air, mumbling something. Sometimes, she mumbled in her sleep; sometimes, she argued and bargained; sometimes, she screamed, *"Get off him," "Not yet."* Osip turned her onto her side and stroked her shoulder. It had to be her shoulder, not her arm, and only in one direction. *"Nu, all right,"* she muttered, and quieted.

He put on the tennis-racket bathrobe Stalina had bought for his last birthday and plodded to the kitchen, from which emitted some kind of music. Katya sat there, looking transfixed. (High? Had it finally happened?) "Katyenok," he said. She jumped, and then slouched herself back into boredom.

"Hey." Katya was still wearing her daytime clothes, and eating the top layer of the Polish chocolate wafer cake the Chaikins had brought over. The chocolate had been poured into curlicues and heraldic symbols, like you were being knighted for eating it. He reached for a piece, but the rackets stretching around his stomach made him pull his hand back.

"I had such strange dreams," he said, stretching and smiling. He wanted things to be cozy between them, but they hadn't been for a long time. "About Galich. No one understands my Galich," he said in his joke voice. She looked interested, for once. "Should I play you some?" he said. She shrugged, but paused her music.

Osip rummaged through the cassettes Stalina had tried, more than once, to throw out, and had finally relegated to a giant ceramic pig.

He turned the tape on and they waited, but instead of Galich's baritone, out came the reedy, hysterical voice of Osip's brother Lev, speaking in his odd British and Russian-accented English about discriminatory university admissions in the USSR. "But vee, the

Soviet Jewry, will not suckle at breast of oppressor…"

Katya smirked. Osip began to render his usual apologia: Lev had spent ten years in the Perm labor camp for saying those things she found so amusing, she should have seen him when they'd first immigrated, President Reagan himself… "We wouldn't even have house without Uncle Lev." Katya rested her head on her folded arms.

He replaced the cassette, and Galich began one of his untitled poems. Osip explained that the hundred-headed monster represented the Soviet government. "In Russia, only very hip people know what Galich is really saying."

"Most people are so retarded," Katya said in a rush. "Like, I like this band, Joy Division? But no one's even heard of them. Just because they're old, doesn't mean they're not good. Like that kid Roman today? He thinks the shit — sorry — on MTV is music."

Osip liked the sound of this old Joy band. It had to be better than those Sex Pistols on her tee shirt. "Maybe you play them for me?"

"Okay," Katya said, tapped the cake knife on the table through the rest of Galich's song, and then shot upstairs. "You can download them, but I don't think that's fair," she said, a little too loudly, on her way back down. She imitated Brezhnev, which she always did when she was in a good mood. *Exports from our petrochemical factories —*"

Osip laughed, but worried that she might have woken Stalina or the other girls. Quietly, he said, "How you can do that, when you weren't even born —"

Katya sat on the stairs with a thud, muttering. It was a strange way to end a joke. After a minute, she got up again, walking more slowly. "Okay, I'm going to play you, like, their most mainstream song, because if you don't get it, you definitely won't get anything else by them." She put the tape in and a man spoke quietly over music, about love, and even though Osip couldn't quite make out what the man was saying, he had a reasonable tone.

"Very good," Osip said, nodding at Katya.

"Really? You're not just saying that to seem young or whatever? Sorry." She looked down and broke off another piece of wafer cake.

"What are words?"

"Okay." Katya re-started the song and said the lyrics along with the man. They were about routines, and ambitions, both of which topics, come to think of it, were lyrically under-represented, even in the oeuvres of the bards. "Very interesting," Osip said during the chorus. It was generous of her, quietly reciting this for him, in her voice that so often sounded as if it were being forced out of a can.

"So maybe we go to a concert of Joy? For your birthday?"

"Uh, the lead singer killed himself in like 1980."

"But, Katyenok, you were not even born in 1980," was the first thing he thought to say. Why would his daughter be listening to suicide music? He scooped up some cake crumbs with his fingers. *"Even Galich didn't kill himself, and you know how he suffered."*

"So?"

"Music should be" — he searched for an English word to make her understand — "motivational." It was the wrong word, he knew as soon as he'd said it, a word from work.

"Now you sound like fu — like Yana, how she's always pretending to love Joan Jett. You want me to pretend?"

He didn't know where to start explaining and put on his joke voice again. "Just because you and sisters don't like same music, doesn't mean you can't be friends."

"I have friends," she said, scraping the cake knife along the edge of the plate.

He took the knife from her hand and cut himself a giant slice. *"Friends are not — you don't want to be like Uncle Lev. You want to have a family."*

She leaned back, away from him. Russian made her defensive; he shouldn't have used it. "That's what you guys are always scaring us with." The next song came on, someone screaming, in a nasal voice, some garbled, unintelligible phrase.

He said, "You want to just live by self? Sit in room and listen to death metal?" The chocolate tasted of gasoline.

"Oh my God, it's not death metal."

"It is. It has death, and metal. Death plus metal by simple equation is death metal." His voice had gotten high.

Katya leaned forward, making one last attempt at explaining the hipness of her music. "He doesn't sing about death. If you just listen —"

He couldn't agree to this death-worship. "A little too much I am listen for tonight."

"Whatever." She turned off the CD player and stood.

"Are you meaning it?" he said.

"What?"

In a falsetto: "I don't need my family, I don't need anyone, I —" He broke off and stuffed another wafer into his mouth.

She sighed and shifted between her large, pink-slippered feet. "I'm always saying something spastic."

He wanted to end on a funny note, so he held his hand out for her to shake. Her hand was warm and damp, like something just born. Who could know what she was thinking? After she went upstairs, he wrapped the cake in cellophane and wandered back to bed. He had a few more years with her, at least.

Stalina

"If you were in Russia..." Stalina's Russian Soul, that blowsy whore, kept whispering, its moist *nalivka* breath coagulating on Stalina's ear and keeping her from sleep.

Stalina hadn't believed in souls, Russian or otherwise, until she was on the train to Italy. Finally, she'd gotten her family permission to immigrate; finally, Osip, Milla, and Yana were all asleep; finally, Stalina's nausea had passed; finally, she could begin planning for their stay in Rome — would those *matryoshka* dolls they'd bought really sell? For good prices? Were Italians really that stupid?

As the train tunneled through woods, she heard an inane lisp: *"Our last chance to gaze at our beloved birches."* She twisted in her seat: no one was awake except for some soldiers, skinny and gallant — they'd insisted on giving up their seats, were standing and smoking and almost mouthing their dirty jokes so as not to disturb the others. They seemed not have heard the voice. All the traitors to the motherland in their soiled going-abroad best (they hadn't anticipated, although they should have, that they would be waiting eighteen hours in the boiling station): they slept so soundly, attached to one another through the shoulder or the ear, like paper dolls, leaning in synchrony through the curves.

Perhaps someone was only faking sleep? That babushka in the fedora, maybe? Playing tricks with strings and mirrors? *"What do you mean, Citizenka, harassing strangers like this?"* Stalina said in a louder voice.

"'Citizenka' — ha! I am the Russian Soul, the firebird in the hearts of all Russians whose hearts still beat."* It was a hallucination, then. That made sense. She hadn't had anything to drink since some brown water from the train station's sink at one that afternoon.

"How quickly time alights from our grasp." The lisp seemed to be coming from her purse, but that was impossible, although, if she were Osip, she would open the purse to make sure the KGB

Nadia Kalman

hadn't planted a radio bomb. The voice began to recite Karamzin. Stalina opened the purse. Of course, there was nothing new inside: a comb, their visas, the sixty-seven American dollars of their savings they had been allowed to wrest from the Great Mother's fist, and a piece of lace she'd taken from her wedding dress at the last minute, a lapse into sentimentality, which was already turning dingy. Stalina threw the lace in the window ashtray. The voice continued to declaim: "*Gloomy nature captures your gentle glance/ It is as if she mourns along with you.*" Only now, it seemed to be coming from the ashtray, where the rag was moving — not moving on its own, of course, just being joggled by the motion of the train. Stalina would sleep. If, that is, she wasn't already sleeping. "*Bid farewell to the birches, whispering of our ancestors, how their swords gleamed in the moonlight, how their horses' hooves would echo —*"

Whispering, so her sleeping husband and daughters wouldn't hear, Stalina said, "*On their way to pogrom my grandmother?*" With an effort, she restrained herself from further speech: they hadn't yet reached the border of the Capacious and Mighty shit-swamp, and also the voice was a dream. In frustration, she tried to pull apart the lace. It felt terrible to do that, almost as if she were betraying Osya…but he always said he didn't care what she wore, as long as she eventually took it off. When he slept, he sometimes looked like a boy, and sometimes, like his grandmother Rufa. Tonight, exhausted, he looked just like Rufa. He stirred irritably at the sound of the lace tearing and muttered something about suspecting the cigarettes.

The lace rose from the ashtray and somehow reconstituted itself into an embroidered ladies' handkerchief of the kind Stalina's great-aunt had brought to funerals, and, upon returning, had opened, to show the family the damp evidence of her suffering. This handkerchief, perhaps a cousin of the great-aunt's, asked whether there were any succor Stalina might offer to ease the suffering of her fellow exiles. Mightn't she lead them in a song of comfort? *Little Grey Wolf*, perhaps? Stalina tried and tried to sleep, and finally slept, and it was wonderful, but when she awoke in the daylight, so did the handkerchief.

Ever since that night, Stalina could not think quietly for more than ten minutes without the Russian Soul romanticizing, moralizing, and, worst of all, attempting to awaken nostalgia for *La Belle Russie*, as if Stalina had ever lived in such a place. People called her hard and irritable, but it was the soul that had made her so. Now, she threw off the satin blanket, which looked better than it felt. Osya snored amiably beside her, also on his stomach, underneath the sheet (long ago they had agreed to split bed coverings thus), his face turned towards her, puffing clouds of innocently sour breath.

"*If only you had remained true to the Motherland, she would have already brought forth a gallant groom for your daughter,*" the soul said.

"*Listen, napkin, we're never going back to those anti-Semites, hear?*" Stalina said.

But. If they were in Boston…Boston: the most European of all American cities, the center of Russian immigrant *intelligentsia*, home to Harvard and MIT, imagine the kinds of suitors for her daughters' hands.

Also, Stalina's mother, in a fit of senile willfulness, had relocated herself from Stamford to Boston the previous year. Now she was hosting *vecherinkas* every night: pensioners drinking, smoking, singing, and at times dancing to old Komsomol songs. If she were in Boston, Stalina could monitor these activities.

And Edward Nudel kept offering her a job in his Cambridge lab, paying more than twice what she now earned. So many *hipovi* Boston boutiques she'd be able to afford — she'd really teach her daughters how to dress then.

But Stalina had had a romance with Edward before meeting Osip, if by "romance," one meant an affair with a stooped, finicky, married and frustrated biochemist, an affair as interminable and depressing as the post-Khrushchev era in which it had occurred, and Osip was jealous. You're standing in the way of your daughters' future happiness, she silently accused the hump.

"*How dare you slander your lord and protector?*" The handkerchief was guarding her virtue again. Stalina wouldn't even bother to reply. She would go to sleep like a serious person.

She took deep breaths. What would be a nice school outfit for Katya? American children had no idea how lucky they were not to have to wear brown dresses every day. Katya would look her best in purple — a sweater? A jumpsuit?

Stalina turned, and turned again, like a body turning under a car. What kind of person is so morbid? she would have asked her daughters, if one of them had thought it.

Stalina's family had been afraid, which had not been remarkable given the time and place. What was remarkable was the means they undertook to remove their reasons for fear. "*Surely, Stalin would never arrest anyone named after himself. This name will be good for our entire family — if anyone ever questions us, we'll just say, 'Me? I love Stalin so much I named my daughter after him.'*"

Despite this and other precautions, Stalina's father, a chemist specializing in sugar, had been fired from his job the year she started first grade. She hadn't been able to understand exactly why. Her first thought had been that perhaps he had been stealing the sugar: it was what she would have done, but it was not that. People wrote newspaper articles calling him a Cosmopolitan, but he was really an Internationalist, which was much better, her mother said. (Stalina wanted to bring these two advanced words in to her teacher, but her mother looked about to slap her when she voiced this gold-medal idea.)

"*Chemistry belongs to all nations,*" was the mock-pompous, hopeful sentence her father intoned at dinner, raising his glass of homemade dandelion wine, before getting on the train to Moscow, where he was going to speak to the boy who used to share a desk with him at school and was now a high-ranking official.

His old seatmate refused to see him. On his way back to the train station, he was hit by a bus. When he got out of the hospital, he couldn't remember anything: not his reasons for going to Moscow, not the risk he now ran of being arrested, not the names of the co-workers and friends who never came to see him. That job was left to Stalina's mother, who whispered, "*He doesn't even know to aim at the toilet anymore,*" and, "*He went out into the street yesterday, no underpants,*" and "*He called me a dirty devil.*" He died in the hospital, screaming for his father to come and defend him from the *hooligani*, the *pogromschiki*, the nurses, the pigeons.

A few years later, Khrushchev made his secret speech and the children at school began to make fun of Stalina's name. "*Foreigner.*" "*I am not.*" "*You're foreign to the spirit of Marxism-Leninism, aren't you?*"

Her mother said, "*Just go by Lina, there are lots of Linas.*"

Stalina refused. Stalin had been evil, but she couldn't fault his choice of a name. He'd renamed himself "steel," and then he'd taken over the Comintern. The name was something to be reckoned with.

And now, here was her husband, right next to her, a nice solid man, and there was her Russia, across the world, years in the past. There was their television, right in their bedroom, there was her Cubist figurine from the Boston Museum, luxuries unimaginable, and three daughters, almost all grown, none knowing how to fix a button or a bribe, nor needing to know.

How Milla had behaved tonight! She'd have to talk to her about how an educated young woman conducts herself in polite society, speaks with young men, grooms her eyebrows, serves the people sitting around her, memorizes anecdotes....The handkerchief agreed, and added other suggestions of lessons, and with this long and satisfying list, Stalina finally soothed herself to sleep.

Nadia Kalman

Lev

The open air makes the smell fly off me and the headache with it. The crows fly off the roof, which superstition says is a sign that either bad luck or money is departing, which brings us to the Jewish Question.

The Affair of the Cosmopolitans, the Affair of the Dictionary, the Affairs of the Doctors, the Engineers, the Theater Critics: Stalin's whimsical purges. Remember the time he accused those Yiddish poets of spying for Israel? Have you guessed what happened to that merry band who traveled the world proclaiming the end of anti-Semitism?

When they weren't trying to establish an American satellite in the Crimea (The Affair of the Jewish Anti-Fascist Committee), the Jews were pretending to be Soviets: Mendelsteins renaming themselves Molochniks! And many writers of the pastoral Ukrainian school of brooks and Masha: circumcised under their kaftans. What right did that Yitzhak so-called Goyko (really, Gavstein) have to sing about our Ukrainian maypoles, our Ukrainian cabbage soup? demanded the vigorous Fourth Estate.

Internationalism: once, the Bolsheviks said that all nations would be equal and welcome in the Soviet Union. Jews — and what greater proof of their effete Cosmopolitanism could there be? — believed them.

Stalina's father, Josef (another lucky name) Kandel supervised the graduate work of an enterprising lazybones who told him to write her a nice dissertation. He refused. Instead of a dissertation, she wrote an editorial: How dare this Kandel boss around the real Ukrainian engineers? What right had he to study our Ukrainian sucrose? The local newspaper lived to disseminate the people's intelligence.

2

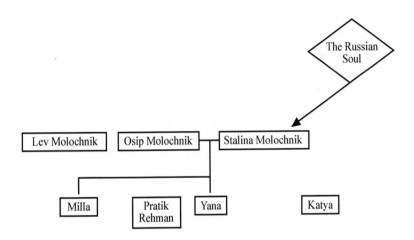

Lev

We skip past the next two years like cats skipping roof to roof. False elections, massacres, poison letters: what is the point of immigration if we are doomed to the same conversations we had in Old Eastern Europe? Haven't we all had enough of history, of the pathetic surprise on everyone's face? (Yes, Petya, it's really you they're going to kill, you've exhausted your allotment of Peace.) I treat history like my grandmother told me to treat dogs, wolves, inspectors, anti-Semites and bees: I don't bother it, it doesn't bother me. You would be happier if you did the same.

The Molochniks, condensed:

Osip's Y2K team dissolved, and another round of layoffs spared him, but took his pension. Stalina got into a long feud with a shiftless sample provider and was deemed insufficiently nurturing by her laboratory director.

Katya ran away to California, because California was mellow and no one there would care about her voice.

Norwalk Technical College kicked Roman out for cheating. He hadn't bothered to hide it: in Nizhny Tagil, everyone had done the same. None of the Chaikins were very surprised. Soon afterwards, Leonid received a promotion and a wonderful new haircut, memorialized by his mother in a dozen photographs.

Milla found a job, right out of college, right in Stamford. Her parents were as happy as she'd hoped, the happiest they'd been since Katya had left.

After many, many visa delays, Pratik Rehman, an exchange student from Bangladesh, arrived at the Molochnik household.

Yana said she was disenchanted with academia, and enrolled in graduate school for education.

In the wake of the events, anything was possible. Despite Pratik's generous and repeated geography lessons, certain members of the Neighborhood Watch continued to ask him about Afghanistan. Katya finally called: she was fine, if they'd just stop looking, she would be fine. She was taking classes, she was doing so much better than she had in Stamford. If they'd just stop looking, she'd call again. Following the example of an influential trance musician who had just done the same, Malcolm proposed to Milla.

Stalina

Milla and Malcolm sat on the couch, looking at the fireplace, the lamps, everywhere but at Osip and Stalina, like coquettes in an Ostrovsky play. "I've been wondering," Malcolm said, petting the stubble on his right cheek, "What's going on with the statues?"

Stalina glanced at the Art Deco figurines arrayed on the bookshelf behind her. Perhaps Malcolm's parents were able to afford more elaborate pieces, but she doubted they possessed her aesthetic courage. Some of her figurines danced in the nude. The Soul said, *"This rogue is challenging you in your own home."*

"No, not those," Malcolm said, laughing. "The ones outside. Yeah, like driving in today, I saw this girl in a leather jacket, right by the mall. But then, I looked, and she was a statue."

"I told him they're everywhere," Milla said breathlessly.

"I do not know," Stalina said. Malcolm hadn't driven in to talk such *irunda*, nonsense.

"Dad? Do you know why they're here?" Milla asked.

"I am hearing maybe something to do with developer's son." Osip, today, would not make a joke about property values: he understood the seriousness of the situation.

"She is as our fertile land after rainfall, or before appending Finland," the Soul said. Today, it smelled of flowery perfume, the kind of perfume that some men would buy and drink. Was it possible that Milla, with all the excellent American birth control available, had still somehow managed to get herself pregnant?

"Okey-dokey," Stalina said, bracing herself.

"We got engaged a week ago," Milla said, glancing at Malcolm with every other word.

"And you are in the position?" Everyone, including Osip, looked at her strangely. She's been trying to translate from Russian, to avoid having to use the only American way of saying it she remembered, a crude colloquialism: "You are sticking up?" Osip gave her a reproachful look.

"Mom, no," Milla said, and then to Malcolm, "She means 'up the stick.'" She and Malcolm giggled because it was very funny that she had such a stupid mother. As soon as she noticed the look on Stalina's face, though, Milla stopped. She probably hadn't meant anything by it, Stalina told herself, as her daughter unclasped her hands to show a tiny engagement ring. "See, Mom, and you thought he'd never want to get married, you said, 'he's not even on five-year plan.'" She was giddy at the thought of having pleased her parents.

Stalina tried to smile. Milla was trying to do the right thing, getting herself married when so many young people just wanted to be swinging in the trees with the other singles. Stalina, in turn, would make the sacrifice of not asking Malcolm whether he had a job, at least not in any obvious way.

Osip's exchange student, Pratik, timidly opened the front door. "I have brought nuts." He put a wax bag on the coffee table.

Stalina said, "So sit, Pratik, we'll have nut party."

"I need to study, unfortunately," he said, heading upstairs. His maroon backpack hit him at every step — what, in Bangladesh they didn't have adjustable straps? "*Don't let the Oriental distract you,*" the handkerchief admonished.

Stalina said, "And so, you get married, it is very nice, and then…"

"I want to have kids, I want to have, like, five kids," Malcolm said.

"Okay, big Jewish family, and in the morning you wake up, and eat balanced breakfast, and then…go to office, or just —" What was the slang? "Or hang?"

Malcolm looked about to laugh.

She said, "It is easy question about future." The handkerchief disagreed: "*It is never easy to divine what will meet us on life's winding,*" etc., and suggested they conjure upon a rooster.

Osip escaped to the liquor cabinet and stood staring at its not very voluminous contents: Malibu, vodka, Manischewitz, and a few bottles of red wine. He patted the bottles, as if to comfort them.

"Actually," Malcolm said after a pause. He now looked as though Stalina's question was exactly what he had been hoping she would ask. "I am trying to choose between these two careers I've been interested in for a long time: law and journalism. So on the law side, I've signed up for the LSAT, that's the Law School —"

"I know," Stalina said. "My girlfriend Alla has niece who's lawyer."

"Okay," Malcolm said, leaning back. "I've also" — he seemed proud to be in possession of that *also* — "talked to a friend of my parents who's going to give me an internship — he's a civil rights lawyer. Should I open this?" He had Pratik's bag of nuts in his hands.

"Excuse for a minute," Osip said, returning with wine glasses. "What is it mean 'internship'?"

Stalina answered in Russian: "*Like Yana had, at the children's club, voluntyorstva for no pay.*" Osip sighed quietly.

"This one is really prestigious," Milla said. "It's more of a fellowship."

"Anyway," Malcolm said, picking out an almond, "journalism is another strong option. I don't know if you guys remember, but sophomore year, I actually ran a newspaper —"

"Yes," Stalina said, beginning to feel nauseated. A two-page tabloid for street people — how do you make money on something like that?

Malcolm nodded, drank some wine.

"Okey-dokey," Stalina said. "But before you tell us you want to be mathematician."

"Yeah, but that was before I took that class, and realized what math metamorphoses into after Calculus, it's a hydra." Malcolm laughed a how-silly-of-me laugh, the kind of laugh only very confident people could afford. If Stalina ever laughed like that at work, people would laugh along with her, thinking all the while: Of course, the woman with the accent made a mistake.

***

After the children left, Stalina sat in the kitchen and let Osip cook some liver for dinner.

"*He's a nice boy from a very good family,*" she said.

Osip nodded.

"*Of course, if we were in Boston, we could bring ten, twenty nice boys to the house for Milla to choose from. But you moved us here, where there's nothing but Leonid and Malcolm. So she picked Malcolm, because he is better-looking. He has longer legs. They'll have attractive children.*"

Osip nodded.

"*He wants to get married, he wants five children, even. That shows he's a serious boy. He will have to make money to support those children.*"

Osip nodded.

"*And you?* Did a cat eat your tongue?" Why did she have to be the only one looking for optimistic things to say? "*What, you think it's better for her not to get married? To sleep with a lot of men, and after that, try to find someone?*"

He stirred the liver as if he were not planning to reply. The Russian Soul counseled "*women's golden patience.*" Why was it that she always had to be the one to face facts? Finally, he lifted the spatula and said, "*I'll teach Malcolm how to do more practical things, fix toilets, like that.*" That was all he could come up with? What about Malcolm's joblessness? Should they try to find him something themselves? Or would that anger his parents? Would he laugh? What would Milla say? She was a smart girl, an accountant, she had to understand…and there was Stalina, in the middle of an argument with her daughter, and Osip nowhere to be found.

For so long, Stalina had felt as if she were driving a *troika* and her daughters were the horses, and she was whipping them forward to what she knew would be a better place. And no one ever thought about how difficult it was for such a driver, how frightening. She said, "*You think Malcolm Strauss wants to learn? To fix toilets? From you? Do you know what his family thinks of us?*"

Osip's shoulders hunched. Now, he had cause to ignore her, and that was what he would do. In a minute, he would finish the liver and take it to the TV room. He would call Pratik in there, too, and Stalina would wander alone through the rest of the house.

"*I said us, Osya, not you, us,*" she said.

Jean

You had to send in the wedding announcement at least two months in advance, was what Bobby's sisters had said. If you were a rapper or a famous banker, like Bobby's cousin Paul, you could get away with five weeks, but that was it. It was now four weeks and five days before the wedding, and no announcement in sight. Part of her wanted only to tell the kids about the deadline and to say, "There's no use now." Another part of her thought Malcolm might still change his mind, so why announce anything? However, she was determined that if Malcolm did break it off, he would have no grounds to blame her. She would proceed with good faith, as Bobby had advised.

"So, have you sent in your *Times* announcement yet?" she asked Malcolm and Milla over take-out Portuguese.

Milla looked at Malcolm, as Jean had known she would. Wouldn't anyone save Pauline from Peril, in the guise of a simple yes/no question?

"Why don't we write it now?" Jean said. "Won't that be fun?" She got a pad and her Waterman pen from her briefcase (Briefly, she wondered about the Waterman Malcolm had received as a graduation gift: had he lost it? She never saw him using it.) "How shall we start? How about, 'Malcolm Philippe Strauss, the son of Jean and Robert Strauss, was wed —" It was difficult to finish the sentence; it made it all seem so real. Now she understood why Malcolm hadn't wanted to write the announcement. "Milla, what's your middle name?"

Milla looked up, seemingly surprised, and pointed to her own masticating mouth. A few seconds later, she said, "Russian people don't really have a middle name? It's the patronymic? So mine is Osipovna."

"So you do have one. 'Milla Osipovna Molochnik, daughter of Osip and Stalina Molochnik, in the Great Hall of the American Museum of Natural History.' Okay?" They nodded.

Now, Jean had a brief respite from Milla, as she and Malcolm filled in information about his family, Yale, ("Weren't you at least cum laude?" she asked. She couldn't believe he hadn't been any laude at all; music was an easy major, wasn't it? At least he'd rowed crew.) his internship with Harold Krasner, and, at his insistence, his "abiding interest in Klezmer music." She needed a few more sips of wine before resuming with Milla. "An accountant's assistant —"

"— Assistant accountant," Milla said. "I mean, sorry, that's my official title."

"Oh, I didn't know that was important. What do you want me to write again?"

"It's not so important...." A little shrug.

"What should I write?"

"Assistant accountant."

"Isn't that what I had? Oh well, 'assistant accountant at Lazar Partners, a Big Ten firm in New York. She graduated magna cum laude.'" She had remembered; Milla should be flattered.

"From Southern Connecticut State," Malcolm added.

"I don't think I have to put that," Jean said. "If I just say she graduated, right after I talk about you, people might think: Yale."

Milla was widening her eyes at Malcolm. What message was this inept Russian spy transmitting now? She didn't like prestige?

Malcolm said, "Southern Conn is a great school for accounting. Everyone knows that."

Milla gazed wetly at Malcolm. Pauline had been rescued.

"Trust me," Jean said. "I'm more experienced —"

"More experienced?" Malcolm said.

"Not like that, you child. I have more experience in the world than you do, and thinking Milla may possibly have gone to Yale will give her that *je ne sais quoi* in people's eyes. Milla, you know what I mean, don't you?"

Milla pointed at her mouth again, as it were too full to speak, but it didn't look all that full to Jean.

Malcolm said, "Aren't we supposed to put in something about you, and something about Milla's parents?"

"How did you know that?"

Malcolm reached for the last prawn and put the whole thing in his mouth, even the disgusting tail. "I read *Sunday Styles* sometimes."

"I thought only homos did that." Jean loved to tease him about being a homo, because he so clearly was not one, although he was not as muscular as she would have liked. "But anyway, I can write that without you. Your father, founder of a law firm, Harvard magna cum laude, blah blah, me, maybe I'll put in that I represented Michael Landon — do you think I should put that in? Do you think anyone would care?"

"Sure, put it in, why not?" he said.

"I don't want it to take up space if no one cares. Do you kids even know who Michael Landon is? Milla, do you know?"

Malcolm said, "Put it in, Mom, it doesn't matter."

"Fine. I'll leave it out." Malcolm sighed and sprawled his legs outwards, as if he were sitting on an exercise ball at the gym, rather than a century-old Louis XV style dining chair, complete with claw feet, that Jean had discovered at an auction in (of all places) Truro, Massachusetts.

Yana

The wedding was in eight days. Milla combed her hair a different way every half hour and stuck a veil on it, stared at herself in the bedroom mirror, refused to emerge. She was becoming a vainer, dumber version of Uncle Lev, not that telling her that made any difference.

From an undisclosed location in Santa Barbara, Katya tortured their mother with her indecision about attending the wedding, bringing Stalina to such a state that she had staggered back from the mall that afternoon cradling a strapless orange prom dress some commissioned witch told her was perfect for a hot M.O.B. Now, the dress lay in wait in its plastic bag at the bottom of Stalina's closet, where she'd let it fall — a very uncharacteristic gesture, alarming in itself — while describing to Yana a dream in which Katya had been a bird playing the piano.

Publicly and politely, as she had done for months, Stalina argued with Jean over expenses, offering to pay for any item Jean happened to mention, be it tuxedo alterations, the rabbi's fee, the entire catering bill (which Yana knew they couldn't afford), or Jean's pedicure.

Privately, less politely, and with a great many more of what Stalina called jokes, she fought — also with Jean, in her mind, but actually with Yana, who was there, over the senselessness of Jean's insistence that the couple be married at the Museum of Natural History, just because a Strauss cousin sat on the board. *"How can you marry young people in the midst of all that death?"* Stalina asked Yana, who felt herself absent during those times, a Jean-protoplasm undulating over her body.

Malcolm fought with his parents over whether he would apply to law school. Yana and Milla fought over whether Milla was a zombie. No one, except for Osip, talked to anyone else unless it was necessary; and no one, except for Yana, laughed at Osip's jokes.

The only unafflicted person in the house was Pratik, who,

having been asked to keep track of invitations and food selections, had created a computerized, color-coded matrix incomprehensible to anyone but himself, in front of which he sat like the Buddha (Yes, Yana knew he was Muslim, but he sat with that air of sated sleepiness, familiar from a bronze figurine in her former lover's office. "Former lover's office" — it sounded so mature, she wished for an opportunity to say it. "Former lover's office" — so breezy, it couldn't possible come from someone who had moved back in with her parents so that her mother would stop her from calling him.)

Now, as the Molochniks and Strausses faced off over table seating, Pratik gave her a look of particular smugness, as if to say, "If my database cannot bring peace to this household, nothing can." The table's mirrored surface multiplied everyone's mouths and chins and noses; there were entirely too many fleshy human parts involved in the discussion.

Yana was trying to keep everyone in line using classroom management techniques she'd learned in graduate school. "Milla will be down in a minute," she said, "but guys? Guys?" She raised one hand in the hair and counted backward to one with her fingers. This was what her professors called a non-intrusive prompt. "Guys!"

Jean Strauss looked at Yana's upraised arm and Yana felt as though it were suddenly too long, and sat down, and apologized. "Milla and Malcolm said before that they want all their cousins to get to know each other, so they wanted them, sort of, mixed." Her own uncertain eyes glanced back from the tabletop. She sat up straight and looked at Pratik. He smiled, as she imagined herself someday smiling at some of the children in her class. He looked as if he wanted to tell her that she just learned differently from the others, not worse.

In jolly tones, Jean Strauss said, "The kids want a cousins' table," and then murmured something in her husband's ear.

Osip said, "Cousins together — very nice, as long as they don't get marry."

Yana forced out a laugh.

Bobby Strauss lifted a forefinger and said, "It's certainly an idea," beginning a measured disquisition on the subject of Strauss cousins, long separated, who would be wretched to find themselves at different tables with cousins not their own.

Only two tables had been planned so far and it was already nine, and the caterer had said she need the seating chart at least ten business days in advance. Yana's stomach hurt at the thought, and she excused herself to go check on her sister. She had been giving the Strausses excuses for Milla's absence since they'd arrived, and now, at Yana's prediction that Milla must be "almost done" with her "work project," Jean didn't even bother to say "hmm."

Milla was sitting in front of the mirror, veil in hand, frowning. She looked as if she were in a commercial for something, that in a moment she would confess her wedding dilemma to a giant deodorant bottle. Instead, she had only Yana, and when Yana asked what was wrong, Milla said, "I just want my hair to be perfect." She'd been saying that all day.

"Is it Malcolm?" If her sister said it was Malcolm, Yana would say, "There's something imperialistic about that guy." But her sister said nothing. Yana said, "If you can't even go downstairs and finish planning your wedding, you should seriously just cancel it."

Milla stood, bent over the mirror, moved a curl from one side of her forehead to the other, and sat back down.

"Are you crazy?" Yana said. She decided to try for a light tone. "Come on, no one cares about your stupid hair." Actually, Jean would probably make some remark. Milla blinked at herself.

Perhaps it would help to explain the larger social justice principles involved. "Do you want people at your wedding to be segregated? That's the Strauss plan, basically." Yana's voice was going to that embarrassing register it had visited many times in high school, trying to get Milla to sign up with her for some extracurricular social justice or blood donation, with the never-forgotten (by Milla) rallying-yelp: "Someday, you'll be bleeding to death, and then you'll feel really bad." Yana had been shy, fearful of the beautiful bohemians of Amnesty International, the upscale elderly of the Red Cross. Milla had always had work, somewhere boring and awful like the supermarket. To this day Yana couldn't understand why Milla would choose that.

Now, Milla said, "People will change their seats anyway."

Yana took a cleansing breath. She imagined Milla as a twelve-year-old student, no, an eight-year-old student. You couldn't be angry at an eight-year-old. You definitely couldn't be angry at a six-year-old. "Okay, look," she said. "It's okay to be scared of marriage. You're pretty young, and it *is* an oppressive construct."

"'Oppressive construct.' I'm not you. I don't care about that."

"If you don't care, I won't care either," Yana said, and walked out, slamming the door as an indication of the seriousness of the issue, and then waited in the hall.

Milla

Hearing Yana leave, Milla twisted her hair into a roll and wound it around the top of her head. If she lowered her face so that only her eyes were visible above the mirror's bottom edge, the mirror reflected a flying saucer.

Milla's thoughts were slow in unfurling, like scrolls, and rhymed, like yearbook poetry. She

Was in love
As of five days ago
With a woman
who was herself
Quite hetero

Julie was a receptionist at the Stamford accounting firm where Milla worked. Only for now, she reminded herself. In just a few weeks, she'd be starting her new job in New York, and she'd forget Julie. New York City was a very exciting place.

But last Tuesday, Milla had been pulling out of the parking lot when she saw Julie lighting a cigarette, and Julie's face, reflecting the flame — Milla accelerated to an unprecedented parking-lot speed of forty miles per hour, leapt over the speed bump and into the traffic circle, trying to drive away from the truth of her love.

For the next few days, she was careful to treat Julie the same as she had before — to be friendly, to be businesslike, assistant accountant to receptionist.

On Friday, Julie appeared at Milla's desk and Milla stopped breathing. Through the ringing in her ears, she heard Julie say that the others were throwing a surprise Bon Voyage party for her. "I know you like to look like natural. But in photos, natural looks like fish reject."

Milla floated up from her creaking chair and shadowed Julie into the empty conference room. Julie had Milla sit on the table. She'd brought a metal suitcase that, when unfolded, resembled a terrifying robotic butterfly. She stood between Milla's legs, and, humming a little, began. Julie's arm pressed against Milla's breast as she applied the lipstick. When it was time for the eyeliner, Milla had to close her eyes, and that made her aware of Julie's chocolaty breath, her tar shampoo. In that moment, she thought Julie might kiss her, but she didn't, of course.

When Julie had used all the colors in the case, she unpacked a final surprise — an expanding mirror — and held it up to Milla's face. Immediately, Milla was reminded of a glasnost-era movie about a hard-currency prostitute she'd seen with her parents. She looked, not like the prostitute-heroine, but like the heroine's hapless Moldavian friend, Glasha, who was trying to move up to hard-currency work after a stint on the streets. Each of her cheeks bore a red triangle. Her lips were red, too, the shiny, bloody red of a recently sated cannibal. Her eyes were almost invisible beneath heavy, downward-sloping purple lashes.

"I love it," she had said. "Can you do it for my wedding, too?"

Julie was Polish, not gay, not wealthy, not even Jewish, not even educated. If Malcolm's parents found out! "Going off with a low-rent Pole, are you?" she imagined Jean saying. Milla would sock Jean right in the mouth (but those pointy teeth), the side of the head, then. Yes, she'd clock her good, grab Julie's hand, and run away to New York City. Not to the Upper West Side, where Malcolm's parents lived, but a more bohemian place: the Village. If Milla's own parents found out —

These thoughts would go away once she was married. At no time previous to this had she been a lesbian. Obviously, lesbianism was one of those things that mysteriously came and went, like a sunspot (Julie's hair in the sun!) or a wart.

She rolled her chair backwards, away from the mirror, so that more of her was visible. A lumpy-nosed vampire, she was lucky, very lucky, to have Malcolm Strauss for a fiancé. "Malcolm Strauss," she said aloud. "My husband is Malcolm Strauss." Then she tried, "My name is Malcolm Strauss," but it sounded all wrong, so she couldn't be a lesbian, or else she'd think it sounded fantastic, wouldn't she?

Her phone rang. It was Malcolm, who had just finished his job interview at an advertising agency whose owner was friends with his mother. "How's the welding coming along?" He called their wedding a welding, because their families were so different.

"Welding is hard work." They were meant to be: they were already becoming an annoying couple. "When are you getting back?"

"I'm meeting Ravi and Jason, so I don't know. One?"

Milla couldn't help sighing into the phone. It was not so easy to live with her fiancé and her parents at once. Her mother would notice how late he'd come back. She couldn't wait until they were married and alone in New York.

"What's that for?" he said. She'd made him feel trapped and defensive, which you were *never ever to do*, all the women's magazines agreed, it was like feeding a Gremlin. "You're not even doing that much, are you? My mom said you just go around saying everything's okay with you."

"I'm sorry. I guess I'm not enough of a *sosh* for you," Milla said and surprised herself by beginning to cry. She felt like a character in *The Outsiders*. Not like a specific character, but like all of them combined: *The Outsider*.

"What's all this?" he said, and it was hard for Milla not to tell him. He was her *sami rodnoy*, her closest person. Instead, she listened as he said, "What's going on?" and, "Milla," and then, as she calmed down, "This is just wedding stuff, right?" and still later, "You think I want a socialist?"

Nadia Kalman

Katya

Katya was living with a guy named Matt, or maybe a couple of guys, she wasn't sure because his friends came over a lot. You have to know what your energy is about. You have to know what your energy is about. Say it fifty times as you breathe out. She breathed out onto the half-open window. There was a time when she would have drawn something in the condensation, an anarchy sign, the mark of the beast, a tulip, but now she looked at it and knew there was no way she could lift her hand and point a finger and make anything recognizable.

Her energy was about the supermarket circular she'd found and reading parts of it aloud to her mother over the phone to convince her she was eating. Katya would have eaten for real, because Matt didn't like her skinny, but the combination of things she was taking — the things it took — made her throw up too often for eating to be worth her time.

A guy flip-flopped through the door. "Still here?" he said, tossing his backpack on the floor. Katya curled her legs up on the window sill. "You're always sitting there, why?" he said with some kind of sensitive thing to his voice.

"I don't know," Katya said. She'd found you could get by with "I don't know" and "Nothing much" and nothing much more. Why hadn't Matt told his friends she didn't like to talk?

"I could just push you out right now," the boy said. Some stupid instinct made Katya grab the frame, so that when he pushed her a few seconds later, she did not fall.

She crossed her arms, stooped her head down so she'd clear the glass. "Do it again," she said.

He looked at her and raised his hand to her shoulder, then laughed and backed away, taking out a cell phone. "Some crazy bitches."

Katya felt a different person take temporary control of her, not Brezhnev, someone else, a window-grabber, a confirmer. She packed up her bridesmaid's dress, called the airline from a pay phone outside. When the feeling ran out half an hour later, she wanted to cancel it all, but lacked the energy, which was how that other person had planned it.

Osip

But they were supposed to be happy! A house before a wedding should be full of giggling and photography. If only someone told him the problem, then Osip, who at twenty-one had published a paper about elevated rails, would find a solution. But in the United States, even in his own family, apparently, his problem-solving abilities, of which one professor, overjoyed to find a smart Jewish boy like Osip at their fifth-rate provincial polytechnic, had called his "sublime pragmatism," counted for nothing.

He stood watering his big lawn like a big — or at least largish — shot, wondering what could be the matter. Here Milla was marrying a famous Strauss. (He'd asked Mrs. Strauss whether they were descended from the jeans-maker, and she'd said yes, and he'd made a funny joke.) Yes, Malcolm was a bit — uncertain, and made other people uncertain as well. Malcolm seemed always to be worrying a decision when he spoke to you, wondering, should he be more friendly to you, or less? Or was there someone else he needed to be friendly to — at that very moment? Osip told himself that he, too, had been uncertain at Malcolm's age. He just hadn't let on: Stalina had been pregnant and they had married. They were in America now, and America was the freedom to admit you didn't know what you were doing.

The rest of the family was jealous of them. Stalina's cousin Valentina had been calling to inform them about the layabouts, the failures, the suicides and homicides who'd graduated from Ivy League colleges.

Stalina liked prestigious people. Stalina liked making others jealous. Stalina liked weddings. What, then, was the matter?

Osip turned the hose on some bushes. It didn't matter if the bench got wet, because Katya was the only one who'd ever sat there.

What would his father have done in Osip's place? He would have waged a successful campaign. He would have been victorious in battle. Osip sighed. Whenever he tried to imagine what his father would do, he found himself, for lack of information, instead imagining what the Commish would do. For the Commish, these family matters would be a distraction from his real work of the week, uncovering a drug ring, say. The Commish's wife would have found it charming that such a tough, streetwise man had no idea when it came to women's problems. She would have massaged his neck.

Katya had come outside, when Osip was watering, when she was nine, ten, and talked to him about science fiction. Osip's favorite books were about feudal civilizations approaching utopia, a nuke for every pod. Katya's books were about psychic girls with silver eyes, teenage clones, robots seeking soulmates. If she'd only stayed for Pratik's arrival, if she'd only learned calculus. Osip had been looking forward to saying: Katyenok, calculus is nothing more than the study of very small numbers.

Pratik

Pratik was a sissy sleeper, had been ever since he, at age six, had shared his bedroom with his asthma-prone grandmother, under strict instructions from his parents to wake them if her breathing changed. Now, anything could wake him: a passing car with muffler trouble, a squirrel in the tree outside his window, Yana, the family insomniac, the family beauty, walking past his door.

He heard her and did what he had not been brave enough to do before: he put on his pants and followed her to the kitchen. He paused in the doorway, wondering whether he should knock, and decided to say, "Oh, hello, Yana," with an air of surprise.

Yana dropped the box of cereal she'd been holding, jumped in the air, and screamed, "Ah," a few times. Pratik closed the kitchen door so they wouldn't wake the rest of the family, hiding a smile at how funny she looked, hopping on one leg like a cripple, her forehead wrinkled like a monkey's.

"Don't do that again," she said. "I'm easily scared, not scared, startled." She picked up the box of cereal from the floor and held it out to him.

"No, thank you," Pratik said. He poured himself a glass of water and sat at the table, hoping Yana would join him.

"This fucking wedding," she said, throwing herself into a chair.

"I wanted to ask you the question, why did you live in New York last year, and not at home?"

"That's an interesting way of putting it," Yana said. "Most people ask me why I moved back here." He loved how her face was always changing. It was comforting, after living with his polite, fearful family, to almost always see what Yana was thinking, even though she most often seemed to be thinking him an arse.

"Why did you move back here?" he said.

He listened to her eating her cereal, which she always had dry. When she'd swallowed, she said, "I was sick of being poor in

the city. I'll have plenty of time to be poor when I'm a teacher."
She spoke those lines like she'd said them many times before.
Somehow, he knew there was another reason. Had a man hurt her,
broken promises? If only she'd tell Pratik, he'd have revenge on the
bandit.

"That is the full reason?" he said.

"What's that supposed to mean?" Yana took a huge spoonful of
cereal into her mouth, and the skin around her lips bulged, making
her look like a sulking child.

He decided to change the subject. "If you have mathematical
projects for your graduate course, I would be happy to assist you,
were you to need assistance. You know," — he knew he should stop
talking, but couldn't — "I was first meant to come here to tutor your
sister." He paused to try to find a clever way of saying that really,
Yana would be assisting him, a debt of tutoring needed to be paid for
the hospitality of her family...

"I'm sure Katya was so deeply concerned about math," Yana
said, cereal powder flying from her lips.

"It is very hard."

"What's very hard, Dr. Science?"

Pratik drank his water. Yana was looking at him as though her
sister's leaving were his fault, as though he'd chased her out the
door brandishing a textbook. That was not Pratik. That was Pratik's
German tutor, the year he was twelve. "It is hard to be without a
family person. When my father was posted to Paris, my mother and
I missed him badly."

Yana pushed her cereal into one cheek and said, "Why didn't
you go with him?'

"I don't know. I remember thinking perhaps he was shamed of
me, because I was always catching up to the language of the country
before. I spoke Spanish with a German accent, for example."

"Did you ever ask?"

Pratik shook his head.

"You should. I read in Atypical Development, one of the main
reasons fathers and sons get alienated is that they feel rejected.
Usually, they don't really want to kill each other, they just need to
unpack their issues."

She was happier now. Although he had no intention of questioning his father, a man so afraid of being held to account that he'd run away from home at age four after having eaten a forbidden *korma*, Pratik said, "I would not know how to begin such a conversation."

"You'd just say, 'Look, Dad, I felt really rejected when you went to Paris without us in' — what year was it?"

Pratik supplied the year, a detailed description of his emotional state, and a theory about the roots of his father's behavior. Yana loved his explanation of the importance of pride for Bengalis, reacting as though the desire to avoid embarrassment were an exotic Eastern proclivity, and supplied I-statements for him to inflict. She became increasingly calm, finally yawning a few times while instructing him to put his anger on the table, or mat, if that was what his family ate upon, and wandered back upstairs to sleep. Pratik cleaned their dishes, touching the glass her lips had touched, giving her a new private nickname: The Anger Manager, TAM for short, and imagining how they'd laugh about it once they were married.

Jean

The night before the wedding, Jean made Bobby rent *Cool Hand Luke*. Paul Newman was so sexy in the movie, but still, every few minutes, she jumped up, wanting to check on something, not sure what needed checking, thinking she heard the phone. She had a headache, and, in the bathroom, stretched the wrinkles back from her face. Was she supposed to feel bad about having been a tan, sexy college student? What was God trying to tell her with wrinkling and spotting and being sued by an ex-client and Bobby's heart problems and this pale and unfashionable sub-European who'd be walking down the aisle tomorrow carrying the Strauss family Torah? Jean had offered the Torah in a moment of weak-minded benevolence upon hearing, back in February, that Milla had agreed to postpone the wedding and get married in August instead of May. A lot could have happened in those extra months, but hadn't. To think: Jean had given money to free Soviet Jews.

"Bobby," she called from the bathroom, "Do you think we should call the kids tomorrow to wake them up?" They were staying at Jean and Bobby's summer house, which was odd. Everyone knew the bride and groom slept separately the night before. Everyone knew about Hamptons traffic.

Bobby shuffled up to the door, not even trying to hold in his stomach. Didn't he realize that her stomach only looked all right because she was always holding her breath? Why couldn't he try to be attractive for her? Either a man should be so naturally handsome, like Paul Newman, that a few blemishes don't matter, or a man should make an effort. She had Bobby, who made a comment: "They have an alarm clock."

Jean walked to her dressing room, Bobby following. "They're kids," she said, "They'll never wake up on time. Maybe that's — okay."

"Jean…" Bobby said.

Jean held her wedding outfit, a white silk shorts-suit, in front of her body. "I should have had Ronette let out the bust more."

"You can unbutton the top, right?"

"It's much too small." Another thing gone wrong. Life was an errand, she had always told Malcolm. What she hadn't told him, but should have, was that errands were not easy. She tried her hardest at everything, and look what happened.

"Try it on," Bobby said. Jean lit her closet and went inside. At her age, she wasn't about to let Bobby see.

"Did you remember to lock it?" Bobby asked from outside, his little joke.

She'd lost a little weight and so only the top button was a problem. The halter drew attention to her arms, still tan from a conference in Cozumel, and to her chest, which looked more freckled than age-spotted. Jean was about to open the door when she caught sight of her back: puffy, pale. She'd have to keep her jacket on tomorrow, that was all. She tugged up the silk shorts (very special for a wedding, Chloe at Saks had said) and opened the mirrored door, then hurriedly reached behind herself and threw on the jacket.

"That looks real good," Bobby said. Whenever he got excited, he spoke like a blues musician. At least she'd distracted him from telling her whatever he'd wanted to tell her before. And an orgasm, if he could manage it, might help her sleep.

"Shall I get more comfortable, then?" Jean said in her best Grace Kelly voice. Stepping away from the closet, she pulled the jacket over her head and threw it at Bobby. He caught it, stretched it out, pretended to play it like a guitar, and then neatly draped it over the bureau. "Good job," Jean said. "Very, very, good job."

Malcolm

Malcolm awoke in his parents' summer house and felt around for his doubts, which he'd discussed at such length with his family, his friends, his rabbi, his barber, his former Ascetic Philosophy professor, this Buddhist guy who hung around New Haven selling stemless carnations, his dentist, and this girl from high school he'd run into at the drugstore. Miraculously, they'd disappeared.

Of course he'd be able to have a band and be married. Of course he'd still be able to hang out with his friends. Milla wasn't jealous. He'd still flirt with girls. The only difference was, he'd have a home girl waiting for him every night.

Of course, marriage was a two-way street. He'd do things to make Milla happy, like cook, and encourage her to be more free, and teach her about music. If Nietzsche had met him and Milla, wouldn't he have said they were those exceptional ones, who could experience both true love and true friendship?

Lately, Milla had looked so different when she was awake, a lumpy vein in her forehead, a wrinkle between her brows. That was probably Malcolm's fault: she could tell he had doubts, or perhaps had even overheard him discussing them. He would do everything he could to match her sleeping and waking faces. He would write her a song.

Milla's lips were small and pink, like a baby's. Sandra had always needed to wear lipstick, had smiled crookedly. In Platonic terms, Milla was better.

Anyway, once he'd agreed with his mother that he had to return to the States, Sandra had disappeared. She hadn't even shown up at the Sydney airport to say goodbye. All this had happened when he was still a college kid. It felt so long ago. Also, Milla would have shown up, closer to the ideal in that regard, as well.

His mother had been right: it would have been impossible to sustain the kind of relationship that makes you want to drop out of

Nadia Kalman

college. His love for Milla was a stable, growing love, a love like moss.

Milla turned onto her stomach. Her hair was still frizzy from the previous night's rain, and she'd be worried when she saw it. He would tell her she was beautiful. She needed her sleep, but he so wanted to wake her up. The previous night, it had been cloudy, and his thoughts had been cloudy, too, but this morning, all was clear. Wake up, love. Your hair will un-frizz and we will be together always. He lay on top of her, lifted some hair off her cheek, and kissed her. "Wake up, beauty, wake up," he whispered. It was a translation from a famous line of Pushkin's she'd recited to him once.

Milla's head jerked and banged his cheek. She was instantly awake. "Sorry, sorry," she said, sprang into action like some kind of fire nurse and ran to the kitchen for ice. "It doesn't even hurt," he said, but let her press it to his face. That was another thing he could do for Milla: let her take care of him.

Milla

Milla sat on an aluminum stool in the Eskimo Room and said, "My wedding," in a perky voice. The room had been closed for several years, and most of the Eskimo dioramas were covered with tarp. In a few places, the tarp had torn, and she could glimpse a hooded head, an upraised arm. She hoped her grandmother Byata would arrive soon.

After a few minutes, Jean Strauss speedwalked in, accompanied by a very tall man with eyebrows like slashes over electric blue eyes, wearing an embroidered robe over jeans. "Meet Dawa," Jean said.

Dawa stuck out his tongue.

"That's a traditional Tibetan greeting," Jean said. "See?" She wiggled her own pointy tongue.

"Nice to meet you," Milla said, standing up.

"Do it," Jean said, and then, "Her tongue's so big. Look how thick it is."

Dawa said, "It will bring your son great happiness."

"Hmm," Jean said.

Dawa grabbed the stools, lined them up in front of the window, produced a tiny silver stereo, inserted an old George Michael CD, and just as George was expounding on the necessity of faith, Julie appeared.

Julie was wearing a navy bustier with diamond buttons in the shape of X's, as if inviting someone to kiss down their length. Dawa and Jean stuck out their tongues. Milla hurried to place herself between them and Julie, saying, "It's Tibetan."

"O-kay," Julie said, a haughty, frightened Polish Valley girl. Milla made introductions.

Julie said, "Is Johann Strauss the relative of yours?"

"Actually, yes," Jean said.

Now Julie was attempting friendliness: "I and all Poland loves waltz."

"Huh." Jean examined herself in the mirror. "Dawa, are my eyebrows balding?"

Emboldened with the need to protect, Milla asked Dawa, "Can we get a stool for Julie?"

"Dear, we have fifteen people about to come through here," Jean said.

"Is okay," Julie said, and guided Milla to the stone bench in the middle of the floor.

"But then how will you —" Julie untied the ribbons on her sandals and kicked them off, knelt on the floor before Milla. "Let me get you a pillow, at least," Milla said. Julie pressed her leg to signal she should stay seated, reached inside her suitcase, and took out a small pillow covered in fiery poppy blossoms. The sight of Julie's lacy thighs amidst the poppies was too much for Milla. She could not look at them again, but then, where to look? Not at Julie's lips, not at her eyes, not her at her collarbone, certainly not at her bustier or those buttons. Milla settled for Julie's left ear, thick and large, but then found herself wondering whether the lobe would be sensitive.

Even though Hebrew school had made an atheist out of Milla (what kind of God would teach near-illiterate Jamie Heisenberg to make up a rhyming, four-part chant about Milla's resemblance to a boll weevil?), she now asked God for a sign. If her long-dead grandfather were to emerge from a diorama and tell her to stop imagining Julie's underpants, then she would have to obey.

Instead, in came her mother, saying, "The show is on road." Yana had gotten Stalina into a business suit, with jewelry, rather than the horrible orange dress she'd bought before. The handkerchief her mother always carried around was neatly folded in the jacket's front pocket, and not (as Stalina had previously modeled it) tucked into the cleavage of the terrible dress.

"Where's Baba Byata?" Milla said.

"Oh, yes, my mother has problem taking the train I tell her," Stalina said in jocularly irritated tones, more in the direction of Jean than of Milla.

As some Strauss cousins entered the room, Yana started. "I have to call the chuppah guy again and…" Scrabbling through her dirty college backpack, she exited with a hasty "Good luck," not looking at Milla.

Julie clamped down on Milla's right eyelash and said, "Maybe you introduce me someone?"

"To more Strausses?" Milla said, as three more Strauss cousins chattered past. But she already understood.

"I want normal American man, like your Malcolm."

"Sure!" Milla said. This enthusiastic response cost her four eyelashes. That was good. That helped her understand what it was like to rip something out. She could still see, couldn't she? That would be life without Julie.

"The only thing Polish have, is kiss your hand. No money, and they cheat." Julie went on: American men were homosexuals, and some of them failed to stand for old ladies on the bus, but they were still better than Poles.

"Now I finish," Julie said. She held the mirror to Milla's face. This being a formal occasion, she had painted two lakes of purple glitter where Milla's cheekbones should have been.

"You made me look really fun. Now, you should get out of here. Go have some fun!" Milla playfully pushed Julie, whose arms were cool and delicately muscled. It was difficult to stop pushing, and Julie almost tumbled over.

Julie stood, squinted. "I put enough powder so nothing come off."

"I know!"

Julie walked away, listing to one side with the weight of her silver suitcase, stockings twisted, fingers glittering purple.

"Dawa can fix you," Jean said, when Julie was out the door. Dawa thanked Jean for her faith. Dawa said that real makeup artists listened to their clients, and fit their soul-talent into the vessels their patrons provided, and that Milla should take him about fifteen minutes.

Jean went outside to get photographed. Dawa told Milla to take a seat in one of the high chairs. Milla couldn't: she was efficiently removing Julie's hideous purple mascara, by crying.

Stalina asked Dawa, whom she called Da-Da, to give them a moment, sat on the bench beside Milla and kicked off her shoes. "*Nu?*"

Milla reached up to wipe her tears. Her hand came back streaked with purple. "*I don't know,*" she said, feeling herself convulse, "*If maybe I...*"

"*If maybe you...*" Her mother leaned forward. Usually, she resembled the Red Queen in *Alice in Wonderland*. Now, her face powdered pink and white, she looked more like the White Rabbit, like someone who understood complications.

"*Maybe — I love someone else. And that other person — I love — more than Malcolm.*"

Her mother handed Milla her handkerchief. "*Nu? You think if Petya Townshend wanted me, I'd have married your father?*"

Milla closed her eyes so that she could see Julie again.

The door opened — Julie? — No, Baba Byata. "*Mam —*" Stalina said.

"*What's this? Who stepped on my little frog? Who?*" Milla's head was in her grandmother's green silk bosom before Stalina could finish her word.

"*Mama, you can stay if you're willing to be helpful. Are you willing to be helpful?*" Stalina said.

"*Of course, I'll help my Millatchka.*"

"*We have only about eight minutes. Our problem: Milla is nervous.*"

"*Of course, she's nervous.*" Baba Byata kissed Milla's hand. What would it feel like if Julie kissed her hand? Milla was a pervert. She didn't deserve Malcolm or her grandmother's bosom, and raised her head, still crying.

Baba Byata said, "*Millatchka, don't you think I was nervous, when I married your grandfather? This isn't the time for bourgeois proprieties, and I must confess that we had already practiced sex —*"

Stalina raised a hand. "*Once more we roll around on the greatcoat in the woods? Now? Really?*" Her expression changed, and she threw her handkerchief on the floor and skewered it on a heel. "*I will not give subtle hints!*" She paused and shook her head. "*You know how I got married? His previous friend showed up and saw I was pregnant. She said to me, such hamstvo, what a little pig she was, 'Six months ago, I was just like you, and Osip left me.'*"

"*Linatchka, you never told me this,*" Byata said.

"*What good would it have done to tell you?*" Stalina turned to Milla. "*Your father's different now, he would never do that. But then, I cried, just like you, except I was already wearing my dress. It wrinkled.*"

"*Oh, golubchik, little swallow, I would have fixed your dress,*" Byata said, reaching a hand out to Stalina.

"*I spoke to myself very strongly. 'Stalina, he chose you. The other one had an abortion. You'll have his children.'*" Switching to English, she added, "He was quite the champion of sperm."

Byata said, "*I'm not allowed to mention physical love, but you can use this charming language on lyagushinka's wedding day?*"

"*Do you want her to have a wedding day? That's it, Mama. That's what the world is. That's how people get married.*"

Milla had somehow stopped crying. "*You think I should?*"

"*Horseradish is no sweeter than radish. Here we've organized a marriage to Malcolm. This other one — he won't marry you, da?*"

"*Da.*"

Her mother stood up, patted Milla on the shoulder, then lunged forward and kissed her on the cheek. "*I left lipstick, tell Dawa.*" She pushed Byata towards the door, paused. "*Or we could be romantic, like the girls in Lermontov. We could get on one of those dinosaurs in the next room and chase him down, that boy you love.*"

"It's okay," Milla said. Her mother didn't really mean it.

Stalina

Stalina stood at the chuppah, watching Milla take those last three steps which proved she was getting married of her own free will. She was glad she'd read that Jewish wedding guide — it was calming to know all the procedures. As the cantor sang the last lines of her song, Osip muttered, "*I should help with the chuppah.*"

"*You — not moving,*" Stalina said.

"*You trust that Johann?*" He gestured with his chin to Malcolm's best man, a bearded Tartar in a yellow velvet suit.

The rabbi said, "I am overjoyed to be marrying this young couple, whose Hebrew names are Moses and Malka." Stalina tried to look pious, even as she thought: Moses and *Malka*? Like a peasant baba? Why not Miriam?

Osip was looking up at the chuppah, suspicion in his eyes, probably wishing he'd gone into the garage and built one himself, and forgetting he was no good at such projects. Malcolm was smiling at everyone like he was about to free them from serfdom.

The handkerchief said, "*If Milla grows consumptive, will it be Malcolm who empties her bloody cups, carries her in his arms to the sunlit veranda?*"

Osip grabbed the pole above Johan's hand, saying, "You will excuse."

Jean looked over at them and Stalina gave her best American check-my-back-teeth smile. Were those really shorts on Jean's chicken legs? It was either in terrible taste or too avant-garde for even Stalina to understand.

"*Trapped by your ignorance of Western ways,*" the handkerchief suggested.

The rabbi said he'd known and loved the entire Strauss family for years. He was honored to have in his synagogue descendents of Oscar Solomon Straus, the first Jewish cabinet member in American history. This new generation of Strausses was also one of trailblazers,

Jean having been one of only twenty women in her law school class, and Bobby having convinced the board of Temple Beth El that the conference room should be repainted not in white, as it had always been, but in turquoise. "Many of our members thought turquoise was too bold, but Bobby said, 'Well, we're a bold congregation.'"

The Molochniks were less familiar to him, and indeed, less familiar to many of the guests, "strangers in a strange land." Stalina eyed Osip to make sure he wouldn't make a joke about the science fiction book of that title, but he was calmer now that he'd commandeered the pole.

A movement at the back — a new arrival — no, not Katya. It was Osip's most recent boss, a bony woman not beloved by any of the Molochniks. Yana had promised that Katya would come.

It was Milla's turn to say the vows. Osip strained forward to hear her, pulling the chuppah off balance. "*A beautiful bride,*" the handkerchief said, "*like a porcelain doll.*" Stalina squeezed it but could not make it get quiet. She could barely hear Milla. "*Will marriage place her high on a proud mahogany bookcase, or will marriage break her into delicate shards, too fine for even a mother to repair, or will marriage melt her, as the heat released by a hydrogen bomb melts even the sturdiest china? Ah!*" Milla walked around Malcolm seven times, as the tradition said she should. She was so gawky. How could she get married if she didn't even know how to walk gracefully in a dress?

However, Milla finished, smiled a little, and now it was time to sign the contract. Malcolm had to put in writing that he would take care of Milla. His parents were lawyers, so he would take it seriously.

As Arkady Chaikin and a member of the mayor's administration came forward to witness the contract, the Russian Soul did its worst: it sang a song Stalina had learned at Young Pioneer camp. She'd had a boyfriend and he hadn't cared that she was Jewish and he was not. Soon, no one would even remember what the word "Jew" meant, was their opinion. They sat at the campfire, holding hands, and joined everyone in singing:

Crumbs of stars
I'll give to you

Nadia Kalman

Instead of a crown
A gentle song

"*And did you find that gentle love you dreamed of?*" the handkerchief said. "*Or did you ruin yourself for the sake of the old bitch Adventure?*"

Milla was staring at her with round, red-veined eyes. "You have to drink the wine now," Milla said.

Katya

In the airplane bathroom, the lights were blessedly dim, and the mirror smudged her into any regular girl. Katya had missed her first plane, and so had missed the ceremony, but should make it to the reception, Yana had said, it would be extremely hard even for Katya to miss the reception. Katya wasn't worried, because she'd taken a few pills.

She put on her bridesmaid's dress. It came with a scarf, which she tied in a bow at the front of her neck. It was like her head was her wedding present.

As she returned to her seat, she felt calm and immense, and also she wanted to die inside the dress. It was a dark pond and to sink into it she took a few more pills. She fell asleep, and when she awoke, she couldn't remember how many pills she'd taken before, so she took one more, and another in the taxi, to be safe.

The museum had three doors, but no people, and she chose the door decorated with violets, and Yana was there. Katya had been right about the doors. She wanted to tell Yana, but Yana spoke too quickly: "Finally. Malcolm's parents showed this movie they had professionally made, called Legally Strauss, I was throwing up, basically, but Mom was crying in the bathroom about how our family was just as good, so can you sing 'We Are Family'? Like you did in that talent show, but without the weird man-voice? It's not the crowd for that. Do you remember the words? Say hi to Milla — they're carrying her on chairs again, with her consent or not, I have no idea." She stopped talking. "You're on something. Right?"

"Okay," Katya said.

"I can get you water. Or coffee." Yana pulled Katya's hair back from her forehead. "If we put you in a ponytail, you'll look more normal. Jesus Christ."

Her father came up and said, arms spread, "We thought you'd

crashed plane!"

That wasn't funny. Her family shouldn't always be expecting her to crash things.

Osip

Osip waited as Bobby Strauss, in a "morning suit" that matched his own (Osip had never heard of grown men dressing like twins before this wedding), finished his speech. "Here we are in the Hall of Advanced Mammals, and I have to say — I'm feeling like a dinosaur." The Strausses laughed. Osip laughed, too, because he was representing the Molochniks on stage. Stalina smiled her approval. She was so much happier now that Katya was here.

Bobby Strauss was talking about September 11. "When all of us felt as though we had lost our innocence, our children made the most innocent decision of all…" Osip couldn't be expected to come up with something about September 11 on the spot, could he? Bobby Strauss, in the meantime, had finished with terrorism and moved on to Judaism, providing an English translation of the wedding contract, explaining why it was a model legal document, pronouncing the word "Ketubah" in what seemed to Osip like an excessively Hebraic accent. He finished: "I hope this marriage endures as long as the eighteenth-century Lodz Torah Milla carried up the aisle." Colossal applause, standing ovations, whistles and a few weeping faces. The Russians tried to clap in rhythm, but broke down in the face of the Americans' chaotic onslaught.

Osip fixed his gaze on some small, smooth-featured horses trotting across a mural. They, at least, looked friendly, expectant of evolution but not impatient for it. "We are so happy Milla is marrying a boy from such a large and —" Stalina mouthed the word *culturnaya* — he remembered — "cultured family. Malcolm, you are like son to me. Milla, you are like daughter." A few people laughed, Strausses, yet.

"Our great Russian bard Bulat Okudjava said about people in love, they are '*Kracivie i mudriye kak bogi, schastliviye kak jiteli zemli.*' In English: 'Beautiful and wise as gods, happy as Earthlings.' This is what I see in Malcolm and Milla, and it makes me happy, also." A few people applauded.

He could stop here, but Bobby Strauss's speech had been very long, with symbolism. Osip could be symbolic. "My company makes surgical staples." The audience looked impressed, or, perhaps, confused. "If you are stapled with our staple, it will be in you until you die. From another cause, not rupture." He turned his head, so as not to see Stalina's expression, and found himself face-to-face with a Strauss grandfather, who was smiling. He was also drooling. Still, Osip felt a little bit encouraged, a little bit understood. "So I hope, my daughter and son, that your marriage is joined with very strong staple. How? You must be design engineer." Of marriage, but also of staples for the marriage, no? He massaged his forehead, trying to organize his thoughts. "You choose a good metal and the shape you want. Then you see if works. If it doesn't, fine, change." What was he saying?

He'd spent so much time telling Stalina it would all be all right. Milla still had her eleven-year-old face. "We should now drink to newlyweds." Everyone drank — almost everyone. Roman, the Chaikin nephew, had his arms crossed and was looking at the guests as if he were about to report them.

Edward Nudel, that show-off, started the chanting: "*Gor'ka, Gor'ka, Gor'ka!*" Bitter, bitter, bitter, the Russians shouted, first the large, rowdy Boston contingent, then the smaller Stamford group. Polya, Stalina's cousin with all the problems, stood on a chair and scratched her arms in time to the chanting. Milla, smart girl, kissed Malcolm on the lips. The American guests looked so confused that Osip, who'd been leaving the stage, returned to the microphone in a pedagogical capacity. "*Gor'ka* means bitter," he whispered over the chanting. "The married young couple must kiss to make our *shampanskoye* sweet. *Shampanskoye* is champagne."

The Russians smiled at one another, bolstered by Osip's explanation, and returned to the chant with renewed gusto. "*Gor'ka, gor'ka, gor'ka, gor'ka, gor'ka, gor'ka, gor'ka!*" Milla kissed Malcolm again and again.

Pratik

"Your first Jewish wedding, huh?" Mrs. Rabinowitz said to Pratik. He was seated at a table with nine Strausses, who had pulled their chairs together to discuss someone's son's potential Jacuzzi, and two Rabinowitzes.

"What a location, huh?" Mrs. Rabinowitz said to Pratik, pointing to a display. "Look at them, fighting over a girl."

"She means female moose," Mr. Rabinowitz said.

"What, you're a biologist now?"

Mr. Rabinowitz looked as though he were about to say something, but only made a quiet sound, somewhere between a whistle and a moan.

"In Bangladesh we have a museum like this, but no one ever gets married in it," Pratik said, watching Yana talk to the keyboard player, a man with a shaved head and pleated neck — a turtle.

Mrs. Rabinowitz laughed, and then grew serious. "Osip told us how you…came to be. Feel free to ask us anything you want. Even if you think it sounds stupid, it's okay."

"Thank you." What could Yana possibly have to say to that man? Perhaps he was shirking his work, and she was reprimanding him.

Mrs. Rabinowitz said, "We were the ones who helped Osip and Stalina when they first got here. We showed them where the synagogue was, and how to use the supermarket —"

"— Not the supermarket, the laundromat —" Mr. Rabinowitz said, chunks of risotto toppling from his fork.

"— And now we're just really good friends." Mrs. Rabinowitz nodded at Pratik until he felt like he had to say something.

"What wonderful luck." Pratik ate a forkful of grotesquely overcooked rice. Yana had moved away from the keyboardist and the band was playing a new song, more pop rock without singing.

Mrs. Rabinowitz wiped her mouth, re-applied lipstick, and kissed the napkin. "I'll start slow, okay? The chuppah is that canopy?" She drew an arch in the air. Couples were coming onto the floor: Milla and Malcolm, their college friends, Mr. Molochnik pretending to drag Mrs. Molochnik by the hair.

"The friends decorate it. For my wedding, my friends hung Snickers bars on it. I said, 'You know I'm eating these, right?'"

Now Yana was half-sitting at the very edge of a chair with the bridesmaids and a girl who looked almost like her, but not as pretty — Katya, the youngest sister, probably, opposite a sloth skeleton. Yana started to get up, and another one of the bridesmaids patted her arm, said something that made her nod and sit all the way back in her chair and take a drink of wine.

"Any questions? Am I going too fast?" Mrs. Rabinowitz said.

Pratik smiled and shook his head. He did have a question, but it bore no relation to Judaism; at least, he hoped it did not. Why didn't anyone know how to dance? Even those guests who were in time with the music had only four or five different movements. Pratik had been only a peripheral member of the bhangra dance group at university, but even he knew twenty-six individual steps and motions. "You are being most illuminating."

"See?" Mrs. Rabinowitz said to her husband, "I'm *illuminating*." She leaned closer to Pratik, "Repeat after me: kugel…"

Perhaps he could teach his dance steps to Yana. She would wear a belt of gold coins and a red sari, she'd be sweating — but why not ask her to dance now? He wasn't his father, shrinking behind doorways of consulates, waiting to be asked. Mr. Molochnik had dragged Mrs. Molochnik out by the hair. Perhaps that was what they liked in this family, a firm, manly approach.

Mrs. Rabinowitz said, "Sour cream, crushed cornflakes, cottage cheese, cinnamon…"

However, in all of the dancing couples, the man was taller than the woman, whereas Pratik was slightly shorter than Yana. Was it just not done here, to have a minor size discrepancy in favor of the woman? An absurd prejudice. Pratik's own mother was a bit taller than his father, and when they were together, they looked elegant, cosmopolitan. Not that they ever danced.

"I usually serve it with pineapple," Mrs. Rabinowitz said.

Yana was still at the table, alone with Katya. No one had invited her to dance, probably because her combination of beauty and intelligence was so intimidating. "All right, old boy," he said to himself, assuming a hearty British accent, like that of the grocer he and his mother had visited in London.

All of us, in times of danger, call forth the songs that make us brave. Those about to be the Most Valiant Heroes of 1971 sang the songs of Kazi Nazrul Islam. Pratik, too, possessed a talisman in lyric form. He allowed his eyes to half close, and imagined Robert Plant rocking, flinging about his curly locks (much like Yana's), singing of his quest to reach a place "Over the Hills and Far Away." Just thinking of the song's ending, the screaming bravado of all those oh's, gave him the strength to excuse himself from the Rabinowitzes and make his way over to where Yana sat. He needed to think through Jimmy Page's entire guitar riff before he was able to tap her on the shoulder.

She turned around, and he noticed that some of her mascara had leaked below her eyes. Had she been crying? Did weddings make her sentimental?

He said, "This must be your younger sister, Katya? I am so pleased to meet you."

Katya's eyes closed.

Yana mouthed something to him, "Can you believe it?" or "Can you see it?" glanced at Katya again, and then said loudly, "Are you having a good time?"

"It is a phenomenon of a wedding. And you, how do you like it?"

"So far, it's been more work than my worst student-teaching day, and I don't know what's next. At least Katya finally got here, right, Katya?" Katya opened her eyes and nodded. "Have more coffee," Yana said.

"Is she all right?" Pratik asked.

Yana shrugged.

"All right," Pratik said, and just stood for a moment. "What were you worrying over before?" It was hopeless: how could any of these limp queries possibly lead to dancing?

"What, now?"

"Before I saw you, it looked like you wanted to stand up, and then your friend eased your worry." Pratik realized he was pretending to pat Yana's arm as her friend had done. His hand hovered above her warm skin.

"You were watching me?"

"I was watching the room around, the exhibits are interested, interesting." How he hated whatever it was that made his English abysmal just when he needed it most.

"Okay." Yana looked back at her plate, which was almost empty. Such a strong, healthy girl, so different from the sticks in his graduate program.

Led Zeppelin had promised: many dreams come true.

"Perhaps after you've eaten, you will like to dance?"

Yana shook her head.

He sagged. "No problemo."

"No, I was just surprised. Sure, if you want to dance, we can dance. I'm not really a dancer." Pratik bit his lip to prevent himself from saying he already knew that, he had guessed, but he would teach her, for hours if necessary. "I might have to go, like in the middle of the dance, if there's some emergency."

"All right," Pratik said, almost breaking into laughter, wanting to dance right there, a courtship dance from the Bollywood movies of which his father disapproved.

Yana stood: so it was going to happen that very moment. He followed her, eyes on the slim trail of hairs at the back of her neck, until they were in the very center of all the dead beasts.

She stood back, looking at him. The band began playing a fast song, something Latin. Pratik had never danced to this kind of music: perhaps the keyboardist was to blame. He didn't know — was he supposed to take her in his arms? Would a double kick-clap be apropos?

Before he could decide, Yana said, "I took merengue for my fascist Movement requirement." She stepped forward, her lips at the level of his eyes. "You step back."

As she pushed him this way and that, his eyes told her lips that he would always do what she said, even if it meant separating himself from her, and pleaded that she never ask such a thing of him. The dance sped up, and she breathed with her mouth: a smell of fresh fish, beloved by both their cultures, poured forth like a promise.

Katya

Katya may have been out of it but she wasn't too out of it to know what she saw when she looked at her sister and that Indian guy. The way he looked up at Yana was the way no one would ever look up at Katya unless they were her children, and then it would only be because they were hungry, her children would be hungry, of course. Although it was a fast song, she was not happy like she had been once in a while at raves. Which was a good thing, of course. At least now Katya could drink some champagne. Before, Yana had covered her glass when the waiters came by.

Her father was looking at her. She smiled and twirled her fingers around the sides of her head like "pa-aarty," but he frowned. She rested her chin on her clasped hands like Audrey Hepburn as a waiter filled her glass. If that didn't reassure him, nothing would. Who wouldn't want Audrey Hepburn for a daughter?

Yana pinched her shoulder. She must have fallen asleep again. "You're up next," Yana said. "All right?"

"Oh, I feel very restored now," Katya said, because it was an Audrey Hepburn thing to say, and because she did feel all right. She mounted the stage, almost bumping into the cute, cute! keyboard player. "Let's go, boys."

As the music began, Katya saw her mother, standing in a little circle of her own, staring at Katya as if Katya were her Barbie Dream House, her mansion. And when her mother saw that Katya saw, she smiled and began shrugging her shoulders in jerky little motions.

Katya opened her mouth, which still felt sour from the coffee, but it didn't matter. She sang about having all her sisters with her and pointed her thumbs to the side, just like the Sister Sledge girls did in the video, only there were no sisters over there.

She sang about everyone getting up and singing, and her mother tugged her father up from his chair, and her mother's mouth opened to sing. Her mother would do anything the song told her to do.

Nadia Kalman

The next few lines were easier, and the dancing felt more natural, now that people in the audience were dancing, too. Milla came close to the stage, shyly bumping hips with her new husband. Even Baba Byata stood and clapped and nodded. The next line was about a family dose of love, and it was telling her she'd been right to take those pills, and the chorus rolled forth like a pill down a hill. High! High hopes they had — for the future, and their goals in sight.

Katya wanted to say they were more than family, they were ancient, they were powerful — "We are mastodons," she sang, and pointed, with both hands, at the brown bones.

"Oh, I can't hear you now." It was strange: singing those words actually made it hard to hear, as if they had cast a spell. Where were they in the music? She couldn't really move around anymore: it was as if she'd been transformed into that hateful fourth Sister Sledge sister, the one with short hair who always had to dance in the back. Her stomach felt too light, and the music stopped, even though she hadn't sung about feathers yet.

People clapped, but not a lot, or maybe she still couldn't hear very well. She tried to jump off the stage but someone caught and lowered her down. Yana was walking over to her. Yana was a good sister, but a bit of a narc. "Ya-narc," Katya possibly said aloud, and then turned around and ran away. At least, she told herself to run, but she could still see her shoes, which suggested that maybe she was not.

"Excuse me, excuse me, excuse me," she heard Yana saying behind her, and then she didn't hear her anymore. Glancing back, Katya saw that Yana had gotten tangled up in a bunch of their grandmother's friends. This was her chance for freedom. She'd just begun to get her share. You didn't always have to go to California. Sometimes you could just step out of the wedding room, and there would be the regular, shut-down museum, familiar whales and polar bears, all doing their own things. It was like California had been in the beginning, restful. The floor was clean and cool. It was calm here — why couldn't it be calm like this everywhere? Everything in the room was asking her to stay.

Roman

Roman couldn't believe that Katya Molochnik, whom he'd thought was so cool, had just sung disco. That was almost worse than the fact that she'd obviously been high.

Everyone else at his table of Russians had shaken their shoulders and jutted their necks in time with the disco song. Of course, as soon as Katya Molochnik had left the stage, they were back to business: asking his cousin Leonid what would happen to oil prices if "we" invaded Iraq. You'd think, if Leonid really knew the answer, that he could just point his thumb up or down, and that would be the end of it, but no. Leonid took his glasses off and put them on again, he shook his head, he gazed off into the hopeful future, he talked and talked. The only person besides Roman who wasn't enraptured by oil prices was a little Polish girl, who kept staring with longing at a table of Americans behind Roman's left shoulder.

A shorty in a *seeski*-squeezing shirt asked Roman whether he was a banker, too.

"Construction," Roman said. The shorty looked away as if he were a drug dealer. "Also, DJ. Romin Tha White Russian." He had recently spun at a teen night at the Jewish Community Center; maybe she had a younger bother or sister who had been there? No, she said.

"Romin is like Wu-Tang Clan. You know?" She exchanged glances with her friend, and Roman gave up on explaining that, whereas Wu-Tang was about Hong Kong-style martial arts, he was influenced by the ways of the ronin.

Leonid drained his glass and began describing a recent trip to Singapore, a place both crazy and efficient.

If all these *Molodoj* had such great lives, then why did they need to drink? A different girl, one who was almost the bomb, asked whether Leonid might look over her retirement plan. "I'm Audi," Roman said, and went in search of a place where a man could smoke.

Yana

Yana checked both bathrooms, the coat closet, the locked gift shop (she wouldn't put it past Katya to break in there), the Eskimo changing room. She walked up and down the hallways, being calm but purposeful, briefly looking people in the eyes, which was the best way to ward off attackers, she'd learned in self-defense class. It didn't work very well. Her aunts tried to spray her hair. Pratik asked her to dance again. Dancing. When Katya could be dying, or having sex with someone really inappropriate.

"Yo, yo." She tried to ignore it, but this voice was attached to a tattooed hand that gripped her arm. It was Roman, the Chaikins' nephew.

"Your sister, your little —" he held his hands at waist-height, as if describing a five-year-old.

"Where? *Gde?*"

He led her to a corner room. The lights were off, and at first, all Yana saw was the walrus family: two parents, two children, heteronormative to the max. A smell of vomit — Katya, eyes open, on the floor.

Yana dropped to her knees.

Katya stirred. "Okay," she said.

"I slap to wake her," Roman said.

"You slapped her?" Yana said. "What the hell?" Katya lifted her neck. "I thought you were just on pot. What is it? What did you take? Was it E?"

Katya shrugged and almost smirked. Now Yana wanted to slap her, too. "Try to remember, okay? It's important to remember what you took. Where's your bag? Let's go to the bathroom. I hope no one sees us. Can you stand?"

Katya reached her hand past Yana's shoulder, to Roman.

Pulling Katya up, he said, "You will break yourself like Chinese cup with drugs."

Who was this potential wife-beater and anti-Asian bigot to lecture her sister? "Thanks. We're good." He didn't seem to understand. Yana took Katya's hand out of his and tucked it into the crook of her arm.

Stalina

Stalina had a stomachache. Osip made jokes, her mother posited seventeen terrifying diseases in the space of a minute, and the Russian Soul extolled mustard plasters.

It worsened as she walked to the bathroom — a terrible dizzy nausea. Osip's aunt Anastasia Arkadeyevna blocked her path, but, as usual, just saying her name, in this respectful form, with an enormous smile, gained Stalina free passage. Anastasia Arkadeyevna called banalities after her, and she nodded without turning her head. She wanted badly to lean against the wall, but kept her distance so as not to be tempted. Her hand was damp, and slipped on the metal bathroom door as she pushed it open.

Yana, without her gorgeous scarf, held Katya's hair back over the sink. Washing her face in the middle of a wedding? Katya stood, and the handkerchief said, *"Takae blednay, takae bednay"* — so pale, so poor. Those words were close together in Russian, and now she saw why.

"What happened?" she said, jerking Yana's shoulder, her stomach lurching with the movement.

"She's okay," Yana said. "She just felt a little sick."

Katya said. "I can sing the song again, if you want."

"She's okay now," Yana said. "Mom, she always ends up okay."

Stalina said, "Why, Katyenok, at your sister's wedding, a beautiful occasion, a time for the whole family…" Most of her words came from Anastasia Arkadeyevna, but Stalina didn't know what else to say. There was no point in asking why.

"An innocent mother would ask," the handkerchief murmured.

"We are leopard seals," Katya said. Her lips were beige, a color for a couch, not a mouth.

"Is it your classes? Bad grades? Yana, what's that look you're giving me?"

"Nothing." Yana began washing her hands.

"I don't like that look. Katyenok, I'd be so happy to help you with your math…" Stalina bent over and put her hands on her knees — no time to run into a stall to vomit. Nothing came. Instead, the handkerchief, quoting both Reagan and Stalina's father: "*Doveryay, no proveryay,*" trust, but verify.

Katya

They were taking her back to the airport, but she was three, she had made a mistake, her father would be traveling with her. She stretched her arms up, but he backed away. She was too old. She hid her face in her hands. She was back in her childhood house, and he was carrying her after all, stooping under the stairs so she wouldn't hit her head.

She awoke in the middle of the night and her mother was scrabbling through her backpack, robbing her. Katya told her she would give her the money if she just asked, not that she had much, but she had her return ticket. Her mother could sell it, she guessed. Her mother crawled up to the bed and tore up the ticket in front of Katya's face. It was ungrateful and mean. She needed another pill, but fell asleep before she could find it.

Cold water on her face. Was she back at camp? Was she sleeping in the park? It was still dark, and her mother was back. She tried to explain that her mother should let her alone until she calmed down and got another pill. She was still mad about the stealing. Her mother watered her with her mermaid watering can. Katya rolled onto the floor. There was her backpack, unzipped, but no, maybe her pocket? Where were her jeans? She'd told her mother to leave, she'd told her nicely.

Pratik

A week after the wedding, Pratik heard a brass-knuckled knock on his bedroom door and opened it to Yana. She said:

Why did you come here?

What are you studying?

Isn't industrial engineering just another way for the rich to plant their boots on the necks of the poor?

When were you born?

What do you think of the dowry system?

What do you think of the class system?

Do you think Kat's going to be all right? Why? What are your reasons? Stalina just found that detox program on the Internet, you know, she and my dad. Do you still think it'll be okay?

Have you had a lot of girlfriends?

Was she really great, then?

Aren't you going to devote any of your career to creating potable water?

Aren't we living in a police state?

Do you think I should take the job in Washington Heights? It would mean living here one more year, so I don't know if it's worth it. Do you think it's worth it?

What do you think of Joe Lieberman? Of Air America Radio? Of Gandhi? Of Rumi?

One night, Yana came not with questions but with explanations: She had been drinking because it was a friend's birthday party, a really good friend's, Lisa's, and Lisa was going to teach English at this school in a fishing village in Mexico. The school was called the American School, but it wasn't an American school, really, that part was bogus, but Lisa was going because she'd grown up there. That was the kind of the thing Yana had always wanted to do, but she didn't know Spanish, and she was happy for Lisa, but she would miss her, it was hard to find people who were real. So they'd had vodka, which she didn't like, but she guessed she'd been trying to remind herself that she had roots, too, just not among the fishes, fishers, fishermen. She held up her hand for a high-five. You know how people said you got beer goggles? Vodka goggles were much worse, believe her.

Pratik, who had never had alcohol, nodded. He wasn't sure of all her slang but he thought he knew the meaning. Yana spun on his office chair, trying to grab the Columbia mug on his desk with every turn. He pulled the chair back and held it until it stopped trying to move. Bending his head to a proper 45 degree angle, like a film actor, he kissed her.

Milla

Malcolm and Milla honeymooned in California, driving from town to town filled with girls who looked like cruder versions of Julie. Milla woke Malcolm up for sex every morning. Sex was an acquired taste. Julie had made her acquire lesbianism, and Malcolm would help her un-acquire it. Back in New York, where the women wore more clothing, it would be even easier.

Her body felt glazed. It was so hot. She bought a woman's magazine featuring an article on twenty ways to make his toes curl, did four ways a day. She called Yana and talked about how much she'd grown up over the past few weeks, how mature and centered she felt. Yana told her about Katya. No one had told her at the wedding, why?

On their last night in California, Malcolm drove them down a curving road, decelerating and accelerating with each turn. "What if we just moved here?" he said.

"Here?" She braced herself against the window frame.

He put a hand on her shorts. "You wouldn't get as many colds."

"I didn't know you liked it so much."

"It's so free — my parents aren't here, your parents aren't here."

She didn't want to be so far from Yana. "Are there jobs?"

"Listen to my girl: 'Are there jobs?' You wouldn't have to worry about that. I'd get a job. I'd play piano in some roadhouse, or do carpentry."

A few days later, having spoken with his mother for an hour and twenty minutes, Malcolm explained that if they moved into his parents' apartment, they could save up money to eventually buy their own house, rather than dropping it into a sinkhole of rent. Perhaps it was his family origins, Malcolm said, but there was something about land-ownership that called to him. His great-grandparents had owned buildings all over the city.

Jean and Bobby met them at the airport. Malcolm and Milla's room — the former maid's room — had been painted in Antique Rose. That didn't threaten Malcolm's masculinity, did it? "Do you love balloon shades? We tried to get a bigger bed, but it just didn't fit, so your bed is a little short, is that awful?"

"No, that's fine," Milla said. "I usually —" She stopped herself; it seemed too personal, but she should have known better, because now Mrs. Strauss was going to get it out of her.

"You usually what?"

Did she have time to make something up? No, it was no good. "I usually sleep curled up, around Malcolm."

"Hmm."

While they'd been away, the Strausses had gotten a new car. "It's German, so I feel awful," Jean said. "Milla, you never told me whether you love balloon shades."

Malcolm gazed out the window, listening to headphones. Milla said, "I think they're great."

"You mean you think they're fine. See, Bobby, we shouldn't have gotten them for the kids' room."

Bobby glanced back at Milla. She wondered whether the collar of her polo shirt was still clean. "Taste is a muscle," he said.

3

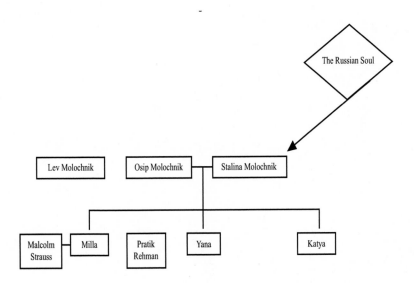

Lev

It seems there may be a war, but it won't derail us. Neither Osip nor Yana could smell the smell, but that was because they sat on the couch and not in my chair. I told them that the war didn't matter, because no one would be coming here; only some of us, and not us, would be going there.

Yana

Pratik was like a first-time chess player: all of his moves were a surprise to his more experienced opponent, that is, Yana. Sometimes that worked in his favor, sometimes not. He kissed her elbow, stuck his finger in her bellybutton. "Wow," he said, as she held his hands above his head. Anything she did, he took as a sign of her odalisque-like prowess.

They met every night at eleven, even if they could still hear gunshots coming from the television. Yana usually came to Pratik's room, but if he got impatient, he would come to hers, coyly peering around her doorframe as if it were a tree trunk.

"I want to say your name in the Russian manner," Pratik said.

Yana burrowed into his quilted blanket. She tried to say it with a Russian accent, but it still came out "Yah — Nah," which was also a summary of her ex-boyfriends' feelings. They had thought that maybe they could love her, but it turned out…nah. It had been like that right up to the fat, uxoriously married, Difference Feminist graduate school professor who'd briefly found her "refreshing."

"Yah-Nah," Pratik said. She pulled the blanket up to her nose.

"You don't like it?" He turned to face her and crossed his legs in their fuchsia pajama bottoms.

"It just sounds kind of stupid. Milla, Katya, those are so nice, I don't know why Stalina messed up mine."

"Guess what your Bengali name would be."

"No." Yana's feet were cold and she stuck them under his legs.

"You would be Yamha, the dove."

"Yeah, like I really have a dove personality."

He raised a bony finger to make some point, but she put her hand, and then her mouth, laughing, over his.

Nadia Kalman

Katya

Katya lay on the couch, trying to read a St. Petersburg guidebook she'd found upstairs. The letters breathed in and out, they blurred themselves, they scuttled into new arrangements. Normal withdrawal, her mother said, so fake-cheery all the time. She wouldn't have to act so fake for much longer.

Russia was the place. How had she not realized it before? In Russia, Katya would tell people her Brezhnev voice was something all Americans did sometimes, to make fun of Communism. In Russia, they had enough problems of their own, no one looked at you except to mug you, or sell you into prostitution, and Katya was a candidate for neither, so no one would care.

Yana said from the loveseat, on which she and Pratik were sitting a careful inch apart, "Do you want to hear something great?"

Katya stared at a photograph of a golden onion dome and wished herself into its warmth. If Yana wanted to help her, she should get her a blanket and some tea, and some pills. If Yana even had a connection, which she probably didn't.

"This'll totally put your addiction slash identity issues into perspective." Yana spoke with too many syllables stacked on one another, like dishes clanking together. Yana began reading aloud from an article about a woman who loved barley. She loved to eat it, and she loved to farm it. She was very satisfied by it. She wanted her people to eat a lot more barley, to start barley farms of their own. It sounded like the barley woman had some addiction slash identity issues of her own, but Katya gathered, from the way Yana was pronouncing words like *fuerte*, that she was meant to be impressed.

Katya would sell her mother's figurines to get a plane ticket. It wasn't anything worse than what she'd already done; it was better, her family could hate her afterwards, and relax. They would regret they hadn't just let her be.

"'Asked about her romantic life, Yadira gives another one of her hearty belly laughs. Barley, she says, is much less trouble than a *novio*. Men can wait.' Isn't she such a role model?" Yana said, threading the fingers of her free hand through Pratik's.

Katya raised her head. "Look at me. Do I look like I need help keeping guys away?"

Yana looked, blinked, began reading again. "'When the *hombres de Kellogg* finally made good on their threat to burn down Yadira's house, she constructed a makeshift shelter in the woods. Now, women of the village use the shelter as a refuge, and, from time to time, a beauty salon.' See?"

Katya thought: If you follow me to the airport, I'll get myself killed right there. She'd make a joke about a bomb.

Milla

As usual, Milla looked at herself in the mirror on the ceiling of the Strausses' elevator. Her face, yellow and angular in the dim light, peered back from inside a black hood. Malcolm had chosen her coat — he had said it made her look Russian, in a good way. She failed again to look as though she lived where she lived.

Opening the door, she heard Jean laughing, as Jean laughed only at Malcolm's jokes. "Oh, oh, oh," Jean said, from the ottoman, and stopped when she saw Milla.

"Honey, you're home," Malcolm said, starting Jean up again. If Jean hadn't been there, Milla would have swooped down for a kiss.

"It's early, isn't it?" Jean said.

"No, I usually finish at, like, 5:30, 5:45." Milla began sweating inside her hood.

Jean opened her mouth wide. "I'm shocked."

"Oh," Milla said, in what she hoped what was a polite, interested tone. She put her bag on the floor and started unbuttoning her coat.

"When I started out, I worked until ten, eleven, midnight. You do what you have to when you're supporting a family."

"I do —" Milla began. Malcolm held his palm sideways, like a Frisbee, and moved it down. That meant she should ease off, she already sounded angry, and didn't she know how that stressed him out?

Milla yanked off her hood. "I actually brought some work home."

"Oh, well," Jean said. "Malcolm, do you want a vitamin?"

"What do I need a vitamin for?" Malcolm frowned and flexed his arm.

"This is a very special vitamin. Your uncle Jeffy swears by it. And he's a homo."

"So I think I'll go work," Milla said. She went into their bedroom and lay on their doll's bed and wrote a letter to Baba Byata.

"*Malcolm's parents feed me very well. Last night, I had dumplings, a kind of Chinese pielmenyi, and a lot of carrots.*" Baba Byata was a big believer in carrots. What else could she write? "*I told Malcolm's parents you said they were very culturniye people, and they were really flattered.*" Milla had done nothing of the kind. ("*Culturniye,* what?" she'd imagined Jean saying.)

She looked at herself in the green mirror that hung by the bed. "We can't, I'm a married woman now," she mouthed to a disappointed imaginary Julie.

She called Yana, who kept giggling, as someone else laughed in the background.

From outside, she heard Jean greeting Bobby: "Why aren't you wearing your other scarf?" and then both of them asking Malcolm to play the piano for them, and Malcolm agreeing, "I have to get back to composing in a few minutes, though." Somehow, Malcolm was able to recreate Barbra Streisand's rendition of the Shema Yisroel, trills and all. He also, following a lengthy explanation, played them a song he'd written. Tonight, for once, he was not meeting up with friends, and his parents were so happy, so grateful, that they forgot to tell Milla when dinner had arrived. She recognized the smell of burnt broccoli — Chinese again — combed her hair, sat next to Malcolm and was quiet as his parents talked about the divorce of a famous author of thrillers featuring the Israeli Mossad (Milla had never read him? Really?), currently being mishandled by a different firm. Malcolm's hand played piano on her leg, as it usually did when he felt like fooling around.

After dinner, he said, "I'm sleepy, are you sleepy, Milly?"

"It's only ten o'clock," Bobby said. "You told me you'd look at the napkin samples."

"Bobby, you know what he means," Jean said. She winked at Milla and Malcolm, which froze them where they stood, hands linked, for a few seconds after Jean had walked away.

In their bedroom, Malcolm said, "So."

"So." They sat side by side on the bed.

Malcolm put his arm around her shoulders. "I hope you're not, like racked with disappointment, that my parents only asked for my opinion on the napkins. I'm totally going to represent both of us when I choose between the little flowers and the medium flowers."

"I know you'll be bringing in the rabbi on this one, too."

"And his minyan, in a minivan." Malcolm flopped back on the bed. "I feel like my head's stuffed with all their minutiae. All the songs I worked on today, they're erased." He flipped open the Stella Adler Studio catalog he'd gotten a few days earlier. "I should just do voiceovers."

Milla lay down next to him. "Did you get a chance to look at that apartment in Queens?"

The apartment was too far out, but Malcolm had met a guy named Jelani, who loved all the same music as Malcolm. They'd grabbed lunch and decided: the two of them would start a multiracial rap-rock-funk band. Jelani was a quarter black, Malcolm was Jewish, and they'd find a Latino guy to play drums and, with any kind of luck, some kind of Asian for bass guitar. The last part was a joke. But the point they were trying to make was serious. The name appeared to Malcolm and Jelani halfway through Indian buffet: Multicult. It mocked their grand ambitions of musical unity, at the same time as it broadcasted those ambitions to the world, balls out. He'd been so inspired, he'd written a new song:

> All the coral mermaids broke off in my hands,
> And the ocean issued its final demands,
> And Landra's gone searching for no-man's land.

"Wait, Landra?" Milla said.

Instead of answering, Malcolm pulled her on top of him and said romantic things any decent wife would have loved to hear. Her breasts, her hair, her shoulders, her thighs, were all deemed more than satisfactory. He had her stand so they could look at themselves in the mirror, whispered, "We'll have to get a bigger one."

Roman

Roman knew some Russian girls, and their thing was to go into Caldor and switch a price tag or two, buy a Sex Dollz tee shirt for seven instead of fifteen dollars. To him, though, there was something anti-Russian in that kind of half-theft.

He was in the book section, where hardly anyone ever went, tucking a GED manual into the back of his jeans, when he spotted Katya Molochnik with her mother.

"*Nu, vot,*" Mrs. Molochnik held up an orange volume. "Go, You Girl: Eating Healthy, Getting in Shape, and Rocking the World. Okey-dokey?"

Katya shrugged and said something Roman couldn't make out. She looked better than she had at the wedding — she was pretty again, in a blurry, bleary way, which was also how she seemed to look out at the book, her mother, the world she was supposed to rock.

He wanted to go over, would have, if not for the books and DVDs concealed on his person. *Had she ever been to the Ivy, in Darien?* he would have asked. *A really hot club, you feel like you're in New York.* His aunt Alla had told him that Mrs. Molochnik was getting Katya off drugs.

Katya shuffled her feet, looking down. "I was never..." something else Roman couldn't make out.

Mrs. Molochnik said something about eggs with tomatoes.

"Maybe just sleep," Katya said.

"*Nu, Katyenok, 'the sun will shine also on our lawn.'*" Mrs. Molochnik put her arm around her. Katya shrugged it off.

All at once, Roman was so angry he couldn't breathe. This girl had what his mother had never had: a whole family to let her live in their house, to worry about what she ate, all that and a bag of chips, and she shrugged it off. All his mother had was him, but she didn't, really, not until he could bring her to the U.S. and set her up right, and when would that be, idiot? He only had two hundred dollars saved so far. He was supposed to have a house for her by now, a car. At least he knew: that was how a child should treat a parent. Not shrug her off.

He tried to breathe. Chillax. She's cute, it's not her fault.

He crouched down farther, pretended to look at the college admissions guides. A guide for insiders, for homosexuals, for top students, for girls, for Latinas, for jocks: all these students were equidistant from him. None of them had his hustle, because none of them needed it. Katya and her mother came to a compromise — Stalina would buy the book, and Katya would try to eat at least one egg. Their voices faded. Roman straightened up and went to the men's clothing section, hoping for a few packs of boxer shorts to resell to the guys on his crew.

Osip

Stalina had many ideas about how to make Katya better. All of them came to her in dreams, and she poked Osip awake and told him, so that at least one of them would remember. "*Osya — castor oil,*" "*Osya — a class in something practical,* "*Osya — White Sun of the Desert, best comedy of any country, no?*" A week after Katya had moved in, Osip bought a notebook. "*Osya — sweaty yoga*" — he'd scribble it down and fall back asleep, notebook on chest.

Osip himself had come up with only one idea, but it was a good one: the beach. At four this morning, he'd checked the weather on the computer — 87 American degrees — like someone saying, "Genius plan." He had immediately left a message at work, taking a personal day. Unable to get back to sleep, he'd packed the car and waited for Stalina to wake so he could tell her, and then another three hours after that, in the kitchen, trying and failing to concentrate on a chronicle of Saddam Hussein's rule in the *National Review.* When she'd come down at eleven-thirty, Katya had said "Okay."

Driving to Shippan, he asked her whether she remembered their vacation at Amston Lake, the summer she was five. "The other girls would be up for beach, but not Katyenok. You liked too much to sleep. You remember how I wake you?"

Silence.

"All I have to say is 'Katya — *bool'k!*'" He made the sound of someone jumping into the water. "*You'd say, 'Bool'k?' and I'd say, 'Yes, but first, bathing suit, brushing teeth...*" Her cheek was pressed to the window and her eyes were closed. "*Do you remember that? Do you remember how I would wake a Katyenok?*"

"Okay." She had Baba Rufa's voice, that voice she'd had at the end of her cigarettes and hospitals.

He turned on the radio. Traffic was catastrophic, everywhere but there: "What you want to do is stay on —" the announcer cautioned. It smelled of seaweed inside the car, even though the windows were rolled up. Katya was too cold for open windows, even though it was 87 American degrees outside.

"Did I ever tell you I have other wife?" he said. She looked at him: that was something. "Yes, twenty years. She is very beautiful." Katya nodded — had she already heard him say this? He finished anyway. "I drive Ford and only Ford for twenty years. Sometimes, other cars beat her a little." Katya nodded. "It's okay," he said. "So I think, maybe Ford can make me their new commercial model? Foxy photo, me on car?"

"Okay," she said, as he pulled into one of a plentitude of potential parking spaces — it was almost empty on weekdays this October. Americans thought if there was no lifeguard, they couldn't swim. He handed Katya the towel he'd brought, the newest and best of the Molochnik towels, having come free with one of Stalina's makeup purchases and featuring overlapping compasses and lips. She held it as though she didn't know what it was for.

"Do you remember how we used to race to the little beach?" He was ready to grab his stomach in two hands and run if she'd agree.

She shrugged.

He said, "You want to race? You think you can beat up me now?"

Silence. She looked like that shivering, pale boy in the painting, *Revelation of Christ to the People*. What had been revealed, to make her look like that? "Look," she said, "I know I'm kind of a heinous problem for you guys. If I go away, like suddenly, to get better —"

Osip dropped his visor hat. "What?"

"To get better."

"Go away — where?" A fat seagull flew over them, a vulture.

"Maybe, like, to Russia? I think I wouldn't be so weird there?" She was joking, so he laughed.

She said, "I'm just telling you so you won't be surprised." She said it was all planned. She felt very positive about this idea. He dug his keys into his palm. The wind stirred up the twigs around their feet, twigs like minnows, he'd thought it would be a day of minnows.

He said, "Don't even think about it."

"You sound like the Commish."

"I'll lock house."

"That never worked," she said, gently, as red bombs floated in the bright periphery of his vision.

"*To leave us again, to go back to that swamp, that whore, that old farter?*" He kicked his car. "What I need this for, if you are run?" It didn't dent: it was a Ford.

"Like, a lot of parents would be happy. Like, I'm going back to our roots." Finally she had some energy in her voice. For this, she had energy.

"*Our what? You know what they call us there? You know what they'll do to a nice Jewish narcomanka like you?*" He wanted to run away alone to the little beach, where no one ever went, to flop down and sleep on its twiggy, black-specked sand. If he ran, she wouldn't follow him, or even stay here. He needed to keep his eyes on her. "*You want to leave your mother again? You want her crazy? Tfu, tfu, tfu. Spit three times over your left shoulder.*"

"What?" She took a step back.

"*So the Evil Eye doesn't hear you.*"

"That's just babushkas —"

"Now!" He hit the hood, burning his hand. She spit, or at least made a spitting noise, with her head turned away. His face was hot and wet. He told her to promise she wouldn't leave.

"Don't you think I've thought — "

He banged on the car. "Promise, promise, promise." His neck burned. She was shivering and he gave her his towel, and the sweatshirt he'd packed. After a long time, she said, "Okay." Was that a promise? What did a promise from her mean? He wanted to ask.

Yana

Yana awoke to find Pratik still on his laptop. He said, "I happened upon a web site. May I read it to you? It would not disturb you?" His cheeks were the color of bricks. He was very angry, and in his anger, more selfish than usual — he began reading before she'd answered. "This gentleman Buford Spelling, a Bangladeshi name, no? He has interesting ideas about our floods which kill us." Turning back around to his laptop, and putting on a kind of British accent, which perched atop his Bengali accent like a crow, he read, "To us Westerners, a house is something important, filled with all our precious belongings and symbols of accomplishment. But poor Bangladeshis have hardly any belongings at all. We must remember that these people have nothing to lose."

Yana said, "What an imperialist."

"It is not that he is an imperialist."

"Sorry."

Usually, Pratik would have now tried to make her feel better about whatever she'd done wrong. Tonight, he just went on. "It is that he is using the tactics of anti-imperialism to claim that we poor Bangladeshis — I am falling over in shock that he does not simply call us Pakis — we are not like the rest of the humanity, we are jolly monkeys in trees, we play with garbage."

Yana tried to massage his shoulders, but they were too stiff. "Where'd you find this?"

"On a website linked to Cambridge University Department of International Studies. This Buford seems to have a connection. He is a chaired professor, for all we know." The tendons at the back of his neck were trembling. "'For the average native, a flood is not that big of a deal.' This is sentence number one. Sentence numero two: 'A 1991 cyclone and flood led to the deaths of over 100,000 people.' No big deal, everything cool. Numero three: 'Westerners should not be overly concerned about these events.'"

Yana said, "I'd beat his ass, if he weren't in Cambridge." Would that be of use? Pratik pulled her onto his lap. Yana hazarded, "Let's see the flood cup as half full, you know? He has no power, he's just writing. You — you're doing things, like that great play…" which Pratik was writing, but he didn't notice the contradiction.

"Oh, I told you about that?" He had, in detail, but she prepared to listen again to how rural schoolchildren would be singing and dancing about flood procedures. Yana kept her eyes looking into his to prevent herself from falling asleep, nodded, uh-huhed like an antediluvian sex-role-dominated sorority girl, and when he finished, they rolled into bed like two slugs and slept through the morning, undiscovered.

Stalina

The Russian Soul waged a campaign of glasnost'. *"You must confess your sins to this tender sapling, or knock-kneed foal, which bends beneath their weight."*

The Russian Soul said, why give Katya cold paper, when Stalina could offer a mother's bosom, a mother's embrace? Stalina had recently found that, if she did not honor it with a reply, it drifted away, bored. However, in her head, she answered that she knew her daughter, she knew how best to tell her, and whom had the handkerchief ever freed from the hold of opiates, that it could advise her?

First, Stalina put the letter in a bag of assorted chocolate mini-bars. What female does not like chocolate? The chocolates disappeared, but the letter endured. It was possible that Stalina had eaten the chocolates herself, during her twice-daily inspections.

Then she put the letter into Katya's laundry basket, but Katya had no immediate plans to do laundry, going around all day in some old safety-pinned jeans and Yana's Take a Bite Out of Shark Finning tee shirt. Finally, one morning, when everyone but the two of them had already left the house, Stalina taped an envelope with Katya's name on it to the bathroom mirror.

Katya

The boy at the check-out desk, who wore a hemp tee shirt and pirate earrings and looked like someone she may have been friends with in high school, made the security guard go through Katya's bag before allowing her to leave. Now she remembered why she'd hardly ever come to the library before.

Outside, a Mennonite girl in a head scarf — had Katya taken physical science with her at Stamford High? — gave Katya a pamphlet about divorce and hurricanes. Elderly, semi-addicted Vietnam War veterans lined the benches, dozily dealing, or arguing with the unseen, or chatting, or sleeping. She reminded herself that the Brezhnev voice hadn't come back for a long time, and she reminded herself that was a good thing.

She'd looked too long. One of the men on the benches unfolded himself and began to limp towards her. Trying to ignore him, Katya took out the graph paper, covered with Byzantine script, which she'd found in the bathroom a week before. She could read Russian well enough to understand that it was addressed to her, and that it was most likely her mother's signature at the bottom. She traced individual letters with her finger. The word "super," in English, appeared once. Was her mother trying to boost her self-esteem again?

The man stood over her shoulder. "Where are you going, girly?" His breath was hungry and Katya knew what that was like. She wanted to tell him she knew, and buy him a sandwich at the Greek place, at the same time as she wanted to run. As was usual for her in such circumstances, she only stood in place. His hand was on Katya's shoulder, like a boyfriend's. "Up to Tittyland?" the man suggested.

"Leave her alone" — but *leave* was pronounced like *leaf*, a Russian accent — oh, no. It was Roman, the Chaikins' nephew.

"Calm down, fuck off, horse shoe, duck luck," the man said. Roman tore the man's hand off her shoulder. The man lifted both his hands and smiled. "The hell you were." He walked back to the bench.

A few of the men on the bench whooped.

Katya shook, but not because of what this Roman, who was asking whether she was okay, may have thought. She had liked the hand. She shoved the letter in her pocket.

Roman's jeans drooped over his white underwear, across the band of which was written Caldor, the name of the chintzy department store a few blocks away. Someone — perhaps he himself — had shaven a thunder-bolt through his hair. "You are okay?" he asked again.

"Yeah." There was a silence. "How are you?" she added, loudly, lest Stalina hear of this encounter and suspect rudeness.

Instead of answering, he said, "And you do drugs or do not do?"

That was all any of her parents' friends asked her. The Russians of Stamford were every one of them treatment counselors. Katya shook her head.

"Yeah?" He grinned and pulled an imaginary lever, and said, "Yes," as if he'd just scored. Obviously, she wasn't about to throw up on him right this second, so what was it with the massive relief? He said, "I am a straight-edge, is underground *termin*. You know?"

"No drugs, no drinking, no meat, no sex."

He dimpled again. "But sex and meat are okay for me."

She looked down.

He said, "Chaikins maybe throw me from house if I do not eat meat like Reagan and Schwarzenegger. Also!" he tapped her arm. "I am now DJ. I am wanting to tell you."

To tell her? "That's cool," she said, although almost every guy she'd known in California had called himself a DJ. Roman nodded, as one who knows he has deserved a compliment. His shirt said "Football! Football! Football!" across the chest.

"Nice shirt," she said, and found herself laughing convulsively. He tugged at his giant jeans. Her bus, like a chaperone, glided towards them down the street.

"Can I have digits?" he said.

The door of the bus sighed open and she vaulted up the steps, lurched towards the back, rested her head on the seat before her, and screwed her eyes shut.

Osip

Osip leaned back in his lawn chair, which Stalina called a director's chair. Osip was, at the very least, the director of beer, and this Friday, he had gotten a Danish brand. Why not? They had saved their Jews. The beer itself was all right, if a bit pale and thin, like a Dane. Galich sang on the cassette player. Katya was safe at the library, living half her life there, just as she had when she was fourteen. She'd always been so serious, and yet, she'd had the worst grades of all his daughters.

Pratik came outside and pulled a chair next to his. "What are you drinking?" Osip said.

"Just lemonade."

"Oh, yes. Sorry." Muslims never drank, which Osip could not imagine. Jewish laws were reasonable, healthy. Who wanted to eat milk and meat together?

"Is that Galich, your favorite?" Pratik said. Osip nodded and corrected Pratik's pronunciation.

"Yes, I can recognize him a little bit. What is he singing about now?" Unlike Osip's daughters, Pratik was interested in the bards.

Osip said, "It is about how one hundred years from today some people will be bored after party and maybe put his cassette in. But cassettes are obsolete technology. Only I have his cassettes, most people, if they listen to him, buy CDs or pirate MP3. For all he was genius, he didn't predict."

"Still, we can hope. People still listen to Led Zeppelin." They sat in silence a few moments, and then Pratik asked him how his work was going.

"It's going," Osip said, pinching a mosquito out of the crook of his arm. "Actually, it is going to India." Osip hadn't even told Stalina this yet. "I am being reassigned." He took another drink of beer. "To genius work of subcontractor database."

"Too bad."

"No, it is Indians who are too bad, right?" Osip laughed to encourage Pratik. "Bangladeshis know."

Pratik smiled and flattened a mosquito on his knee.

"How is school?" Osip said.

"One of my professors is having us design emergency procedures for hurricanes." Pratik frowned at the clear, darkening sky.

"Oh, a *praktika*, very common in engineering school in Russia." Osip was being kind. Designing an "emergency procedure" was hardly the same as designing a thermal waste disposal plant.

"Yes, and if it's all right, I would like to give you my recommendations. I am designing specifically for coastal New England."

Osip had another drink of his beer. "In Connecticut when we have hurricane it equals just rain, boring, not like in Bangladesh." Sometimes, this boy made it hard to relax. Osip decided to steer the conversation towards more philosophical realms. "Mosquitoes," he said, pointing to the bug-zapper, "How many you think die? Is it right that we kill them? If they could kill us, they would kill us. They are only too stupid."

Pratik said, "Have you ever heard of the Long Island Express?"

Osip spread his hands. What now? "Of course I have heard."

"The Long Island hurricane of 1938?"

Tomorrow, Osip had to go to work, face Call Me Evelyn and her operatically amplified constructive criticism. Some people, they could hide in their ivy towers, not he. "Long Island is not Stamford."

Pratik smiled. "You're right. I might be a bit of a control freak, Yana said so the other day."

A mosquito of a thought hovered next to Osip's forehead. "Yana?"

"Yes, she even wrote a song, to the tune of 'Superfreak,' by disco artist Rick James." He laughed and tapped his sandaled foot: "'He is very organized, his tasks completed like no other.'"

Osip said, "My daughter sings many songs for you?"

"No, no. You know Yana is very busy with school, we just bumped into each other in the kitchen, once." He scratched his nose, which was a liar's giveaway, Baba Rufa had always said.

Osip opened his second beer.

Pratik laughed, for some reason.

The Commish was often blindsided, but always recovered quickly. He was older than Osip, and still, he could run from a restaurant, a fried squid dangling from his lips, and apprehend an entire gang of drug thieves. If this Ali Baba had been romancing the Commish's daughter, under his own roof, the Commish would use this time to extract information, subtly. "So, in Bangladesh, how many wives your father has?"

"Oh — he and my mother are actually in Belgium now." Pratik took a gulp of lemonade.

"Oh, so for Belgium he has one wife only. But how many are awaiting him in Bangladesh?"

Pratik said, "It is not, actually, a part of our cultural tradition, polygamy."

This was where the Commish would try a different line of questioning, catch him off guard. If only Pratik drank — but it was all right. Osip had twenty-five years and Soviet military experience on his side. "So, Pratik, my friend, after you learn how to be Muslim James Bond" — Pratik gave him a questioning look — "to resolve all emergencies, you will be moving to Washington to help Bush?"

"Ideally, I'd like to work to help people, especially in my country, Bangladesh —"

"I know your country is Bangladesh."

Pratik swiveled his head around. "Quite a few of these mosquitoes about now, perhaps we —"

Osip held up one hand and lumbered over to the bug zapper, flicked it on "high," and returned to his director's chair.

"In Bangladesh, your wives will sit at home, they cannot go outside without you?"

"Mrs. Molochnik," Pratik said into the screen door, "may I help you with dinner?"

"She can't hear you," Osip said. "When cooking she talks to herself. Women! They are crazy! It is stupid to let them have school, yes?"

Pratik sat up straighter, huffed. Osip had finally managed to anger him, probably by mentioning multiple wives, which had made Pratik envious of his wealthier relatives and their harems.

"I must study," Pratik said. The screen door slammed against the outside wall.

By the time Osip finished his third beer, he'd realized that this little *pisher* probably just had a little *pisher* crush on his Yana. Who could fault him that? At Pratik's age, Osip had already had four women, whereas this boy had the aspect of one of those Komsomolsk kids saving himself for a new kind of marriage, the focus of which would be large-machine repair or hydroponics.

Bobby

Bobby Strauss was, as his wife liked to say, a man of simple tastes. Here he sat before the simplest and tastiest taste of all — a Burger Connoisseur hamburger, no ketchup, no nothing — a truly good burger did not need any condiments, he'd explained to Malcolm before they ordered — and suddenly the series of actions required to eat it seemed too complex. He needed NASA's Command Central, he needed a wire in his ear, like Bush, he needed, well, he needed Jean. Someone besides himself should have heard this most recent of Malcolm's surprises.

Malcolm had immediately resumed chewing away at his cheeseburger, with pickles, mustard, ketchup, lettuce, two kinds of cheese, mouth half open, like a child.

It fell to Bobby to say, "That's wonderful," and then, "She is going to…see it through, isn't she?"

Malcolm paused in his eating. He couldn't have forgotten what they were talking about, could he? "Yeah, of course."

"Good," Bobby said.

"I wrote a song to it already."

"A song, well —" Bobby relaxed enough to tear off a bit of lettuce from his salad. They were back in a familiar place. "Is it going on your demo?"

"I'm not sure. I just wrote it a few nights ago, after Milla showed me the test."

"Oh, the test? Did she take more than one? Did she see a doctor?" Jean was speaking through him; finally, he'd accessed her frequency.

"Just a test."

"So you don't really —"

"She's pregnant, don't worry about that." The waitress was filling up their glasses during this proclamation, not that it made Malcolm lower his voice. Neither Malcolm nor his mother cared, really, who heard them. Bobby wondered again what it was like to feel so right about what you said.

He cleared his throat. "So, you're putting that song on your demo?"

"No, I told you just a second ago."

"Do you remember the words?" The lettuce was fresh, thank God for that.

"Let me think." Unhurriedly, Malcolm took another bite of his cheeseburger. "Something like, 'You are my sun, I am your moon, when all are gone, I'll still be true.'"

Bobby nodded, as if thinking deeply. "It has a certain…" Why had he asked? It was very difficult to respond to Malcolm's music; Malcolm distrusted compliments, and debated criticisms. Perhaps simple observation would be best. "It's simple," Bobby said.

"I was trying to be simple." Malcolm scratched his jaw.

Bobby had a sudden thought. "When you say 'sun,' — is it a boy?"

Malcolm spun a fry in ketchup. "No. We don't know. Milla doesn't need to get the test, because she's so young."

Feeling strangely competitive, Bobby said, "Your mother was young, too, when she had you. Twenty-five." He had been thirty-five, and even at that age, which had felt so ancient at the time, he hadn't been sure he could do it. From the minute Jean had told him, Bobby had felt like a piano had fallen on his head, just as pianos fell on the heads of people in the funnies in his childhood, and the piano had wedged there, and now he had to carry it to work, back, everywhere, every day, and not let on. And now he had to say, "Of course, I was thirty-five."

"I know."

"You feel up to it? You feel ready? Do you have anything saved up?"

"No, but you know, babies really aren't so expensive."

"Oh, no?" Finally, Bobby felt as if he could eat. He took a bite of his burger and it was still good, even though it had cooled. It had passed another test.

Malcolm said, "Yeah, like, we're not going to, you know, send it to private nursery school or get it a *nanny*."

"So one of you will stay home?" He was saying exactly what

Jean would have said, and this would help mitigate her anger over not having been told first.

"I planned it all out already. Like, Milla will take the baby when I'm rehearsing and doing shows, and I'll take it when she's at work, and you guys can take it when we go out. You know what it's like? It's like, when he grows up —" Bobby noticed but did not comment on the "he" — "I'll get him an instrument, if he wants to play, but I'm not going to, like, get Jim from the music store to come to his camp and play two different kinds of keyboards so he can pick the one he likes, in front of all his friends, you know?"

"You adore that keyboard." Jean's words, but not helpful ones. Stick to facts. "You still have that keyboard. You still use it." After years of meditation and medication, he got angry so rarely that it took him a moment to realize. The keyboard, he'd always thought, had been a wonderful present. Rather than choose one himself, Bobby had shown respect for his son's musicianship by having him choose, right on his birthday, which took place at camp, because why wait? It was a music camp, after all, and Malcolm should have the best equipment possible, had been Bobby's thinking. And now he felt Jean's voice coming through him most strongly. "So you felt embarrassed, is that it? Poor little rich boy?"

"No, it was fine. It was an okay —" the fact that Malcolm was leaning back, the fact that Malcolm was smiling, the fact that Malcolm was about to teach him something, the fact that Malcolm still hadn't learned —

Bobby said, "Because why not send Jim away, then? Because why not give it back?"

"Dad —" Malcolm gestured with a half-eaten fry.

"Because it must have been weighing on you, all these years. The chosen unwanted keyboard."

"It was fine —"

"You can't do that with a baby." There. He was done. He looked up to see what Malcolm would do next — storm out? Appease? Fight? Flight?

Malcolm was, at least in this sense, his father's son. "No, I like the keyboard, I like it."

Milla

Jean and Bobby had gotten tickets to see *Fiddler on the Roof* with some friends, and then both they and the friends had gotten incredibly busy. Would Malcolm and Milla like to take advantage? Wouldn't Milla's parents want to come along?

At the theater, Milla sat at the edge of their little group, in case she needed to run to bathroom. The girls who played the sisters were beautiful, so she couldn't look very closely. (She was going to be a mother, after all.) She spent the musical thinking about a recent accounting scandal. Would she, Milla, have had the courage to send a memo comparing a company policy to group masturbation, could she have been an accountant-heroine? She worried about it through three marriages and a pogrom, knowing the answer all along: no. Malcolm would have to be the model of bravery for their child.

On their way to a steakhouse her father had chosen, her mother didn't say anything about peasants eating cows, which was the first sign that something was wrong.

"So," Stalina said, as they came in, ignoring Osip's attempt to help her out of her coat, "this Fiddler is big education for me."

"Oh, yeah?" Malcolm said, looking for a place to throw out his gum.

"Oh, yeah." In her mother's accent, the phrase sounded entirely different; also, louder. "For example, I know now why American ladies say when we arrive, 'Look, is shower,' 'Look, is toilet.' Why are they telling me with such big smiles? Are they engineers who built the toilet? No, they think this is first toilet we ever see. They think we came out of shtetl fighting over if horse was mule. We were *intelligentsia*. We argued over religion and political life, not like here, here people say, 'Never talk about politics or religion.'"

"That's true," Malcolm said, leaning in to match Stalina's posture. He was taking a class in community journalism.

Milla tried to get her mother to move closer to the bar, so that people could more easily pass by them, but Stalina didn't notice the people or Milla's hand on her sleeve. "They think we are only talking *spletnya*, who marries who. We had bigger fish. Who is in jail? Who is losing her job? Who is expelled from party, who is making protest, who is printing *samizdat*? You know how we decide to immigrate?"

"Yeah, I mean, I think so," Milla said.

"Guinness?" Malcolm asked the bartender, who raised his eyebrows in some kind of commiseration.

"To show that we are free people, and not afraid of the worst punishment. And then they take us to supermarket and expect that we will have fainting over food. Five different kinds of apples." Her voice reached a higher pitch. "I will now give blow job to Jimmy Carter."

Malcolm looked at Milla. And what's that for? she wanted to say. Your mom says worse things, just without an accent. She rubbed her mother's padded shoulder.

"*Shto bilo, to bilo*, what was, was, but we can still eat, right, Stalinatchka?" her father said. "Maybe you feel better if you eat." He tried to catch the attention of the woman who assigned tables, by waving at her back. Milla wondered whether she should go try to talk the woman, but didn't want to leave her mother.

Her mother said, "And these women, they bring me their old *chulki*, stockings, stretched out, torn, not washed and I am supposed to say, 'Thank you, thank you, in Russia we had no such things, only skins of bears for legs, teeth for control top.'"

Malcolm nodded. "You wanted new pantyhose."

"No," Stalina almost shouted. "That's like this Fiddler, ' If I were a rich.' We never were thinking, 'We come to America, streets are gold,' we come for freedom, not pantyhose. I can get new pantyhose on black market."

Malcolm nodded again. See? he seemed to be saying, with his unfolded menu, with his comfortable thighs in the barstool, it can all be easy.

"And all the time I wonder, what do they see when they hear: Soviet Union? Onion domes, maybe, icons, maybe, nuclear missiles, maybe. But no. They see little Jews in little towns with cows. I never even see a cow in my life."

"I saw a cow in first grade, once," Malcolm said. He was about to tell the story of how the cow had licked him up and down like a child molester.

Stalina gripped her handkerchief between her fingers. "We, we were intelligentsia, we thought we would come and tell people what it was like, we would give lectures like Uncle Lev."

Milla had been thinking of what to say. "But, Mom, no one's trying to give you pantyhose anymore. We're Americans, we have citizenship, all that stuff was bad, but it's over." Malcolm nodded. Her father didn't look up from rubbing her mother's wrist.

"You think?" Stalina said. "If we are such American pies, why is no table? We are waiting already ten minutes."

"It's a Saturday night," Milla said, lamely.

Osip snapped his fingers, but they made no sound. Malcolm took another sip of his beer, stood, and returned a few minutes later, "It's all fine."

When their waiter arrived, red-haired, casually apologetic, "Table's almost ready, do you know what you want?" Stalina had to turn away, madly making up her stained, ruddy face, and it took three tries for him to understand she only wanted water now.

Osip

Stalina greeted their guests, *"Young people in the house, a jolly group."* She hadn't lost hope in Leonid as a potential husband, for Yana, this time. She hurried everyone out of their coats. Yana and Pratik came out of the kitchen and Katya wandered downstairs, looking sleepy. Yana looked slightly too awake. Her tee shirt had something to say about micro-loans.

Roman Chaikan came into the house smiling, stuck out his hand: a nice boy. Osip resolved to alert him, later, to the fact that his underpants were showing.

Stalina herded them to the dining-room table. Alla Chaikin sat next to Osip and talked about immigrants. *"They want everything in Spanish, did we come here and speak Russian to the street signs?"* Osip, who'd heard this before, and made all possible jokes, put pickled radishes on her plate.

Carrying in the roast, Stalina said, *"Lenya, how's the skiing? I see you've developed many muscles."*

Leonid blushed. "I don't get to do it as much as I want, since my promotion."

"Again a promotion!" Stalina said. Alla smiled, listening.

"I will carve?" Pratik said, and took up the knife. Osip nodded his agreement, although Pratik had never before asked to do that.

Alla said they'd recently been to Boston, demonstrating against the estate tax. *"I have to tell Stalinatchka — but she's busy — we had dinner with the Nudels."*

"Okay," Osip said. He wasn't sure why, exactly, Alla was so jubilant in sharing this news about his wife's former lover. Even here in the U.S., where his name sounded funny, and where he'd immigrated at an age when right-thinking people retire, Nudel had somehow scraped together a big lab.

"They couldn't go on the march, his gout...but anyway he said he got a grant and could triple Stalina's salary if she joins his lab."

"How does he know what my wife makes?"

Alla's orange eyebrows shot up and she took in a mouthful of pickles.

Leonid told a long story about a malfunctioning ski lift in Germany, and the amusing questions his buddies had asked the operator.

Pratik, whose talents did not lie in carving, said, "I personally do not need any kind of machine to climb a mountain. In Bangladesh even small children climb mountains without any machine."

"In Russia, too," Roman said.

"Yes, it is not difficult at all," Pratik said, attempting to saw through cartilage.

Yana smiled strangely.

Leonid returned to his colloquium with Stalina, who admired his charms in an increasingly loud voice.

Having reached the conclusion that the Molochniks, like many reasonable people, preferred her son to other conversational topics, Alla spent the rest of the dinner happily and productively.

Katya

While their families shouted and laughed around them, Roman was asking Katya, "What's your big secret? I know you have," which no one had asked before.

And Katya was saying, to her own vast surprise, like one of those cartoon characters crawling across the desert, moaning for water, suddenly handed a pogo stick, an oasis in a single bound! — "Another voice comes out of me sometimes."

Jean

When she was pregnant, Jean had moved furniture in and out of their new summer house. She'd applied for, and won, a position at a prestigious law firm. She'd gotten a part in the annual New York Bar Association show, a roast of an Italian attorney general, playing the part of his young, expectant mother. She'd danced across the stage holding a salami and singing about how her son would be "an attorney, in general."

So when Milla stood in the entrance to Jean's office, waiting for the world to offer her a chair, and said, "Maybe today's not the best? I feel a little…" Jean had no patience.

"Don't you want to be prepared for your baby?" she said.

Milla nodded dumbly.

"Sit. Please." Jean had to finish filing or she'd never remember where she'd left off, but she was so flustered by the sight of this gormless child about to bear a Strauss, it took so long to remember where everything was, that in the end she just left it like that, saying, "In an hour, I'm taking a deposition, so we have to be very efficient, don't you agree?"

Milla said, "Sure."

As they walked, Jean told her about a fabulous brand of baby food they were selling in the department store just a few blocks away. It was organic, of course, but everyone was saying their products were organic these days. Did Milla know about the different types of organic produce?

No, she did not, so Jean had to explain about genetic modification and heirlooms. It was all hazy in her mind — she was recalling facts from an article she'd read last month. Milla, as a prospective new mother, should have known more about these matters than Jean did. Jean did not know everything; however, she read. Before she could catch herself, she was asking Milla, "Shall I get you a subscription to *Town and Country*?"

This offer gave Milla, magna cum laude alumna of Southern Connecticut State (please!), the chance to say, "I don't really read magazines?" and smirk when she thought Jean wasn't looking. "Could we walk a little more slowly, please?" Milla said.

"Of course." Jean looked down at their feet. Milla's were barely visible, but Jean saw enough to realize she was wearing her eternal penny-loafers. Some women thought pregnancy gave them a free pass on footwear. Jean didn't believe in free passes. Her shoes were heels, four inches. Her feet inside them were gnarled trolls. "Have you finalized a name?"

"Yes, actually."

"Oh? Oh." Malcolm hadn't said anything.

"If it's a girl, Isadora. If it's a boy: Isidor." She sounded peculiarly proud of her sissy boys' name.

"Hmm…" Jean said.

"For Isidor Strauss, the Macy's guy? Remember you said once that you were related? I looked on the Internet, and he was really heroic his whole life, not just on the *Titanic*."

"Of course," Jean said, "Yes. You should know it's not really discussed in our family. We try to be more modest." A silent minute later, she said, "I thought we'd start here," opening the door of her favorite French textile boutique. "We can buy sheets for the crib — won't that be fun?"

"Sure," Milla said.

"This is the kind of store," Jean went on, guiding Milla through the pillows, the rough silks, "where you tell them what you need, and they choose for you. Have you ever been in a store like that? We'll just let them know you're expecting — not that we really need to let them know. They can see you. And they'll say — 'Zees one here, for you,' or 'Zees one is horreebleh.' All vite?" She'd somehow slipped into her mother's Yiddish accent.

Milla said nothing.

"Is this fabulous?" Jean said, holding up the tiniest vine-patterned blanket. No blankies here, only blankets. "Or do you hate it? You hate it." She replaced it in its cube.

"It's — nice," Milla said.

"You're like a Hebrew slave in the lion's den!" Milla looked up, startled, frightened, how else? She was a rabbit in a net, a lobster at the moment it sees the water boil. The saleswoman looked up, too, and Jean gave her a smoky June Allyson laugh.

"Jean?" Milla said, and Jean knew what was coming: Milla was eternally surprised, but incapable of ever surprising. When Milla pointed to her feet it was, of course, because her water had broken, and now it was up to Jean, again, everything hard was up to her: to apologize to the saleswoman, to hail a taxi, to yell at doctors, to call everyone and say, "Guess what the stork dragged in?", up to her again, all of it.

4

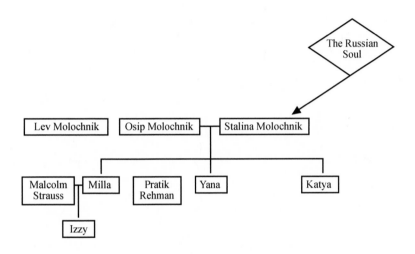

Lev

Osip came with a prospectus of leaves: bronze, silver and gold. For our parents, he said, we will get gold. He's looked at the others on the tree of life in the synagogue and our parents are the most heroic by far. The closest anyone comes is a Myron who loved the law. He wants his baby grandson to understand the grandeur of his history.

Osip's parents were heroes of the Mongolian frontier, mine were enemies of the people. His marched off to defend our impregnable borders; mine also marched, before guns, to a prison camp. His could have appeared in a textbook, for a few years at least, before orders came to scissor them into the dustbin of history; mine were but two of the legions of enemies of the people. His surpassed mine, because his were my invention, in the years following their arrest.

The stirring tale of the death of Osip's parents, Captain Solomon and his faithful nurse: The Mongolian hordes were climbing the walls of the field hospital, our parents threw inkwells on their heads! Then, I turned eight, and the inkwells turned to pistols they fired, two pistols to each parent, and yes, Osya, they safely evacuated all the patients before finally succumbing to a bomb, but don't talk to Baba Rufa about all this, it will only upset her.

It was a wonder to see a Jewish boy who could still believe like that. "*That boy lied about papa, let's beat him up,*" and, of course, the "*let's*" was a joke: it would be me, sitting away the hours on the liar's chest, while Osya worked up the courage to swat him across the cheek.

I later had the chance to learn what Gendela and Solomon must have been called in their last days: wicks. In Russian, *fitliks*. A quick, sharp name for what was left of them, a name to keep us from bothering with the gone.

What, Stalina, is the Point of Immigration, if not new stories?

Katya

Under her umbrella, Katya read the child-rearing book she'd gotten Milla from the library's twenty-five cent rack. "When can I start taking my baby out of the house?" asked the top of a page. The answer was that you could do it immediately, as long as you completed all the items in a checklist that filled the following three pages. Milla would like the checklist, Katya thought; although, perplexingly, it was meant to have been written, or perhaps dictated, by a baby: "Fill ma tummy wif a light meal." Giving Milla the book would also demonstrate Katya was fine, that she was thinking of others, making purchases like an adult, that Milla could stop calling now, especially since she would be so busy with the baby's checklists. It thundered, as if in rebuke for Katya's unsisterly thoughts, and began to rain harder — she closed the book, light flashed at her from all sides, and then Roman stood before her, his face shining.

He took her to the Greek restaurant behind the bus stop. "You look better," he said, like a doctor. He didn't ask her to explain what she'd said that night at her parents' house. He gave her his pickle.

"You can read Russian, right?" Katya said. She put her mother's letter on the table. Roman pushed his souvlaki over to one side, although he hadn't yet finished it. She should have said, "No, finish," but she couldn't wait anymore. Her mother was a biologist. Perhaps she'd had an idea about how to make Katya normal. He began translating.

Do you know why we call you Katyenok, kitten? Your father used to say, girls crawled into my heart, like kittens into a bed, quoting one of his everlasting bards. Isn't that a nice story? What I have left to tell you is not so nice.

"Maybe we should stop," Katya said.

"For reals?"

She reminded herself that she barely knew this guy, she didn't have to see him again.

"Have some of your Coke, at least," she said.

"You are my mom now?" He grinned and sipped in a way that seemed grossly suggestive to Katya, and then, to her relief, resumed translating.

I thought you would grow out of it, like Milla grew out of her allergies, or that a doctor would help you. Remember those doctors I took you to? Back then, my English wasn't good enough to explain the problem. We can go back. My English is "super" now.

The year before you were born, we'd been fired for trying to emigrate, which meant we could get arrested as parasites, and hardly anyone was being let out, and your father — nu, I told him we were too poor for his samizdat games, but his brother Lev was his big hero, Lev, who'd already gotten himself into Perm. I kept your father home during those not-so-secret meetings, refused to let him near a mimeograph, but he insisted on informing the authorities about their "multiple constitutional violations."

Some friends of mine suggested I talk to this man who wrote speeches for Brezhnev, Vladimir, not a Jew, obviously, but sympathetic. "He's ideologically pure," my friends said, "so don't go whining about repression. Talk about your children. Appeal to him as a woman."

I appealed to him as a woman. He appealed to me as a man. Do you know what I mean?

Roman looked up. "You want to go hang at my house?"

He was different from everyone else, big and blonde, robust as a worker in a metro mural. His preposterous faith gave him a vigor no one else had. We were all exhausted from running in zigzags, and he was gliding past in a chauffeured car.

He liked to read to me from the speeches he was writing for Brezhnev. He said he needed to taste the words on his lips. Brezhnev was a famously dull speaker, and Vlad himself was a dull writer, but his faith prevented him from realizing that.

The USSR was the world's strongest and most technologically advanced country; could its condoms be any less so? That was how he thought. Soviet condoms were so leaky, your father's political friends thought they were a government plot to make more Soviets.

Side by side on the bus, Roman and Katya both laughed a little. Roman kept his eyes on the page and Katya stared out the window, at a woman walking behind a supermarket cart loaded with lumber.

I kept quiet. I was greedy, I wanted another baby.

Whatever is wrong with you is a result of my sin. Some people would say "sin" is too serious a word. Your father had some adventures of his own before we were married, you know. That I'm a good wife now, that I make so many good decisions for the family, does that make up for what I did? 'No,' you'll say. 'So,' you'll say.

Why did fate punish you for my sin? Katya, I would give my arms and legs for you to be cured. Your father would put me on the couch every morning, and I'd spend my days eating through a straw and smiling.

However, we live in a world of hard facts. After much thought, I've come to the conviction that our solution lies in carrot juice. I'll squeeze it for you, like I did for your sisters back in Russia. You were born here, and the doctor said Gerber and I listened. (It sounded like a Jewish name.) The lack of carrot juice weakened you in your early years. We'll work up to six glasses.

Roman lay on his bed in the Chaikins' basement, his feet, in red socks, propped on the wall. Katya sat on a pillow on the floor. That she had actually hoped Stalina had concocted a cure in her lab only showed how out of touch she was.

Roman put the pages down and she felt him looking at her. Who wouldn't be curious? She was grotesquely handicapped.

"You are alternative," Roman said.

She laughed, but not really. The least she could do was get out of his house.

He got out of bed, turned his back to her and took off his shirt. He took off his jeans. He took off his red underpants. "Okay?" he said. He sat on the bed and patted the space next to him. It was just like a new immigrant to trust like that. She might have a knife, a camera, a bomb, fangs.

She sat. He touched her cheek.

She did what men liked, her one move, but it had served her well: she closed her eyes.

Yana

Yana drove past the statues she'd always connected with homecoming: a woman and a baby in a carriage, waiting complacently at an intersection where there'd been four accidents in the past two years. It made her think of Milla. For years now, Milla had been keeping something from her, but Yana still had no idea what it was. Nowadays, when Yana called her, Milla talked only of Izzy. It was as if she believed that the more boring baby stories she told, the better a mother she would be.

When Yana pulled in the driveway, Pratik ran out the back door, wearing her father's barbecue apron, with the words Fire Chief across the chest. Or rather, the words would have been across the chest, but the apron was too large for Pratik and so they bestrode his narrow hips: "ire chi." She almost laughed, but he looked very serious.

He rapped on her window like a traffic cop. "I have prepared a surprise feast for our dinner," and then he ran ahead of her, back into the house.

"Kat?" she yelled upstairs, once she'd gotten inside, but Pratik told her Katya was at the library again.

"Sit," he said, and his voice sounded like hers at the beginning of class, when she wasn't sure whether the kids would obey. She wanted him to sit, too, so she could tell him about some revisions to the classroom gum policy she'd been considering, but apparently, this meal required all the china in the house. He flew back and forth from the kitchen. "Kheer is what we have for dessert on special occasions, but alas, or, happily! It is ready before the kalia. So. We will first have the dessert, and then have the meal, like Australians."

"What's this, pudding?" Yana said.

"Yes, it is exactly! It is rice pudding." Pratik stirred his spoon through his bowl. Yana ate a few bites without speaking; it was very good. "Mmmm," she managed, feeling suddenly exhausted, and hoped that would suffice. The pudding reminded her of bedclothes, of a beanbag in the corner of her classroom, she was so lucky that people had designed all these soft, yielding things in which to sleep.

Pratik's mood was livelier. He jumped up every minute or so, apron flapping, to check on the kalia. "You're acting like Jean Strauss," Yana said.

"Ha, ha." Pratik raced back to the kitchen, returned with the kalia in a fish-shaped dish the Molochniks used for gefilte fish. "Ta-da!"

"It looks good. Relax." Yana dug in. He'd put a lot of peas into it, remembering they were her favorite vegetable. She looked up when she realized Pratik had had the same forkful of kalia suspended before his mouth for some time.

"What is it?" she said.

In the silence, she knew. He was breaking up with her. It had been a while, and she'd forgotten the signs. Given their situation, he couldn't merely mumble that he needed his key back, as the professor had. He needed to live in this house with her and couldn't afford to piss her off. So he was going to buy her off instead, with a meal. So he thought.

"Prepare to celebrate," Pratik said. Very clever: he was taking a feminist approach. Perhaps he would quote *Their Eyes Were Watching God*. She pushed her plate away.

"Allow me to introduce you to the new Earthquake Preparedness Coordinator for Bang-Aid!" Pratik finally took a bite.

"Let me guess: you're leaving town."

"Yes," Pratik said. He didn't have to sound so exhilarated, but he probably no longer cared about her feelings, if he ever had. To think of all the time she'd wasted, blathering about him to Katya, when she should have been listening to her sister, helping her. She wasn't really at the library today, Yana knew that, and had known on other days Katya had made the same excuse, but hadn't bothered to learn more. She was probably back with her old friends. Pratik was talking on and on. "...feel I must return to my fatherland."

"How patriarchal of you." When she missed him later, she'd remind herself how empty and conventional he could be.

"You know they will not let me stay here, even if I want. I've applied to more than fifty companies, Yana, you know this, no one wants to give me a visa."

"My dad was right. You should have studied real engineering, like him."

Pratik's chin retreated into his neck. "I am happy to return to Bangladesh. Bangladesh can be a wonderful place for a family."

"Fatherhood in the fatherland."

"What?" he said, but didn't bother to find out. Instead, he began digging under his apron. He wouldn't dare to ask her for a goodbye fuck, would he? He pulled out a brochure. "Here, for example, Chittagong." When she wouldn't take the brochure from his hand, he pushed it across the table.

Bending her head so he wouldn't see her face, Yana read aloud: "'This romantic city combines the busy hum of an active seaport with the shooting quiet of a charming hill town.' That's great. Shooting quiet. There's nothing like a bullet to put the, the heart at ease." She wasn't being as funny as she wanted.

"English is not their language. Don't worry about the language, just look at the picture and tell me what you are thinking."

"I'm thinking. Water, boat, restaurant. You could probably live there until the next flood. Make sure your next girlfriend comes with a flotation device. Silicon — "

"Oh, no, Dove, that is to say —" He jumped from his chair and knelt in front of her, the apron billowing around him like a tent, burrowed under the apron again, pulled out a small box, opened it — a ring. He was rocking back and forth, and the ring trembled on its cotton bed. Yana threw the chair out from under her and plopped to the floor next to him, partially under the table, which cast a shadow over both of them, and reminded her of being little. As a child, she'd longed to crawl underneath and surprise her elders, to grab a leg or untie a shoe, but Milla had been too well-behaved to join her, and Katya had been too small. She put a finger to his chapped lips. He stilled. They stayed that way until they heard Stalina's car in the driveway, and then, Yana dropped the ring into her bra.

Osip

Stalina crossed her arms. Yana crossed her arms. They had only to bend their knees, and they'd be dancing the Kozachok.

Pratik took a seat next to Osip on the couch. He was pale and sweaty, which Osip appreciated. At least Pratik realized how unwelcome his proposal was: I am here to beg that your daughter's hand travel with me to the Third World, where it will be chopped off for committing an infraction of one of our many nonsensical laws.

"You want children Jewish or not Jewish?" Stalina said.

"We're not going to say." Yana squeezed her face into an imitation of Stalina's frown and shook her finger, "'You have to go to synagogue.'" When had Osip and Stalina ever forced the girls to go to synagogue? Only to mark the anniversaries of their grandparents' deaths — did Yana begrudge those visits?

Pratik raised his hands. "We are just meaning we do not want to be like Ayatollah Khomeini, outlawing Baha'i. We will love our children even if they are Baha'i."

"*You hear that, Osya?*"

"*I hear it, what do you want me to say?*"

"English," Yana said.

"In English, your papa and me are Ayatollah." She crushed her handkerchief in her fist, always a sign of trouble, and turned on Osip. "*If we didn't live here, v' dikoi provinceeye, in the wild provinces, if you'd let us move to Boston, your daughter would have a chance to meet interesting boys. Now here she's stuck with your Arab experiment.*"

"Arab — " Yana said, and Pratik looked up. She took a breath. "You wanted another Malcolm? Another rich New York lazy-ass?"

"Malcolm is from good Jewish family, and they have good Jewish baby Izzy."

"Like that's a big deal for us. Your dad was a Cosmopolitan, hello?"

Stalina stepped back and almost out of her left shoe. Her bird chest moved up and down. Osip stood. "Don't ever," she said. She stared into the blank television. "Your grandfather was Internationalist. He knew he was Jew. He was proud. He was a Cohen." Stalina spread her fingers in a vee shape.

"Was he a Dr. Spock?" Yana said under her breath.

"Not all Jews can do this. He was dreaming his grandchildren are praying in Jerusalem, in temples where only Cohens allowed, not running to Bangladesh."

As if she were teaching schoolchildren new and difficult words, Yana said, "We. Are. Getting. Married." After a quick glance at both of her parents, as if that was all she needed to see of them, she said, "We don't care what you think."

"That's it? You don't care?" Osip said. He looked at Pratik, whose fearful eyes perhaps mirrored his own. Osip put a hand to his forehead and stared at the carpet. It was supposed to look like a zebra's skin. The stripes were at a twenty degree angle from the fireplace.

"We would want your blessing —" Pratik said.

Yana lifted a hand. "The right to choose who I can marry —"

Stalina said, "What do we say to such a daughter?"

"Do you care or do you not care?" Osip said.

"She cares, Mr. Molochnik, of course, we both —" Pratik said.

"I don't want you say it, I want she say it." He sounded as if he were still fifteen, trying to buy vodka with a breakable voice.

Yana said, "I'm a Care Bear."

Osip ran from the room and out the back door.

It was raining, but he ran until he reached the red maple — his own beautiful, exotic tree — behind the garage. Under its semi-protective canopy, he could try to forget. He would stay until his regular family had reclaimed the house. Osip had been the father of three girls who jumped on him when he came home at night, who loved his stories about computer programming and youthful *hooliganstvo*. Yana used to sit in that very tree, reading about her crazy activists. Perhaps he should have talked to her back then, but he'd thought that in America, children should be allowed to read any kinds of books they liked. Why else had they come?

He heard a splash and turned to see Stalina's legs in their pink jeans, picking their way through the swampy lawn.

"*I'm in slippers, I can't go all the way out,*" she said.

"*So go home, you're giving all the animals palpitations with your noise,*" he said, and turned away to face the neighbor's fence. The neighbor, Vick, a former alcoholic, grew tomatoes and rode a motorcycle. Why couldn't Osip have a life like that?

She sloshed toward him. "*What animals?*"

"*Hedgehogs, frogs,*" he said as she came near and ducked under the tree's branches, tore off a vine which had had the misfortune of falling across her face.

"*See my slippers?*" She lifted a muddy foot in the air.

Osip gave an elaborate shrug.

"*Don't worry about Yanka, she doesn't know what she's saying. That Arab's probably feeding her hookahs.*"

Osip realized one of the main reasons he'd married Stalina: she was a girl who wouldn't make him cry, who talked about preserving your nerves, who wasted no feelings unless death or career failure were involved. Crying was something Osip had done more of as a boy than any other boy he'd known. And here it was again. Even Stalina, in such moments, couldn't keep him from it. Recidivism would always rear its ugly head, no matter what the liberals said.

"*What am I going to do if you go crazy?*" Stalina took her handkerchief from her pocket. "*Blow.*" He waved it away. "*I'll get them out of the house, and then I'll make you tea.*"

Holding his nose, Osip shook his head. "*You didn't — you didn't say love — so it must — I've raised — I've raised —*"

"*Oh, what have you raised now?*"

Her skeptical tone made him almost angry enough to stop crying. "*Daughters who have only contempt for my teachings!*"

"*You have teachings now?*"

"*You can mock me, too, I don't care anymore.*"

"*You're suddenly a Nihilist?*" Stalina had not actually said that, but he felt her thinking it, and adding something about him being older than Turgenev's Fathers, and mentally younger than the Sons.

"*Why don't you go home?*" he said.

A displaced seagull flew above the tree, and Stalina ducked her head. She had a speech: Seagulls: Not Romantic Birds, as We Were Led to Believe. "*Not without you,*" she said.

"*Why are you trying to make me feel bad?*"

"*Osya.*" She dripped and stared. He would have to go back.

Like an alien spacecraft, Yana had torn the roof from his house, and there was no more warmth, only the feeling of someone watching. Once they were inside, and the children had left, he told Stalina these ludicrous imaginings, and she didn't laugh at him, but seemed to want to say with her eyes, *Don't look up, then.*

Katya

She came carrying a bottle of water, because wasn't that a good thing for a girlfriend of a guy working construction to do?

"Kotletka," Roman shouted over the noise. A kotletka was his favorite food, a chicken patty, so it had become one of his nicknames for her. The sight of his giant silver-toothed smile went to her head.

"*If we approach the blight of imperialism in a more systematic way —*" She turned around and clapped her hand over her mouth: the familiar feel of her own lips wetly moving.

A yellow-gloved hand on her shoulder. "What?" Roman said in her ear.

"The voice." She wasn't going to yell it: he should know by now. There were guys only ten feet away.

"The what?"

"The fucking voice," she said in his ear. "Now your friends hate me."

"But they couldn't fucking hear it. Because it's so" — he spun a finger in the air, "fucking loud."

Katya let herself be turned back around. A few men were looking at her, but in a friendly, leery way, as they might have looked at any girl.

She leaned against a beam and watched him hammer. She'd never spent any time watching construction work before, except for in music videos. "Can I try?"

Roman only had to show her twice. The hammer wasn't very heavy at all. Holding it, she felt like a giant with a long, strong, swinging arm. "You really like?" he said, and found her a mask, and put his gloves on her hands, and warned she'd have to Audi if his boss returned.

After a few minutes, she took off her mask and yelled, "This is easier than I thought." He gave her a thumbs-up. "Will you show me how to drill?" He nodded again, a smile pushing up his mask. "Is this so easy for everyone?" He shook his head. "What's this smell — wood chips?"

"Hot stuff, mask on face," Roman said.

"Fine." She finished the board. "Can I do another one? *We are a unique state requiring unique* —" she covered her mouth, swiveled her head. No one was looking at her. All that banging and sawing sounded like electro-thrash, made her feel like she was back at that non-alcoholic club she'd gone to freshman year of high school, before so many things were her fault. She let her hand drop.

Roman

Roman, having recently discovered a few calling card tricks, dialed his mother's number as soon as his aunt and uncle left for work.

"What up?" he said. He'd taught her this bit of American English before he left.

"*Allo, Allo?*"

"What up?" In the background, Alyosha said, "*kakoita bandit?*", some kind of bandit. Alyosha — the boyfriend who gave her heroin, a gangster so small-time his street name was also the name by which his mother called him.

"*It's me*," Roman finally said.

"*Romachka!*" Something clattered.

Roman said, "*I'm getting all kinds of medals in school.*"

"*Gold or silver?*" She sounded all right, she could follow a conversation.

"*Mostly gold, but a few silver. I tried to send one to you, but the post office told me it was too heavy.*"

"*It was too —*" His mother yelped, and Alyosha came onto the phone.

"*So, boy, you found a baba?*" he said.

"Yeah. Pamela Anderson."

"*It's good to have a baba.*"

In the background, his mother said "*Lyosh,*" laughed.

Roman said, "*How is she?*" Who else could he ask?

His mother took back the phone. "*Roma, tell me something new, something happy.*"

She'd made this request so often, he instantly thought of a half-dozen new lies. But he didn't have to lie about everything anymore. "*I have a girlfriend, she's very nice, she's not wild.*"

"*Is she Jewish?*" His mother, who had conceived him with, to the best of her recollection, an Armenian at a Feast Day disco, wished to know whether this young lady was of the faith.

"*Yes, Jewish, from a good family, friends of Aunt Alla's.*" .

"*She's not spending all your money?*" She didn't sound as happy as he'd thought she would.

"*Mam, no. I've saved over eight hundred dollars.*"

"*You're buying a car? He's buying a car, Lyosh.*" Alyosha snorted into the phone.

"*Mam? Remember, I'm saving to bring you here, to rent you a nice apartment?*"

She sighed. "*Ah, da, and didn't I tell you, I don't need your America? Lyosh, stop it.*"

"*Why don't you just come for a visit and see?*"

"*Your aunt decided you'd luchi pajivyesh, live better with her, I said all right. You weren't fighting to stay here in the provinces with your mother.*"

"*But —*"

"*Zaskuchalsa, got homesick, fine — and live like that. You think I would be so sad and sick all the time if you were here?*"

"*What's he telling you?*" Alyosha said in his lord-of-the-house voice.

"*Don't you want to come here, just for a visit, just to see what it's like?*" Roman said.

"*I don't know.*" She began to cry.

"*Mam: we could go to New York, we could look at all the stores.*"

"*Maybe. Just to look at my son.*"

Alyosha said, "*What kind of shit — bossing you?*"

She muffled the phone for a minute, and when she returned, said, "*No, Roman, you really can't boss me.*"

"*I'm not, mam, you just said —*"

"*I'm the mother. I'm the mother, hear?*" What did Alyosha have her on now?

"*But —*"

"*Oh no, you're not the czar.*" She hung up.

Malcolm

After Milla and Izzy finally left for the park, Malcolm and Jelani tried to rock, Malcolm on the keyboard, Jelani on the guitar, and Malcolm was the one who knew a lot more about music, but he kept missing cues.

"Boy," Jelani said. Malcolm hated it when Jelani called him "boy," but today, he deserved it.

"I probably just need to eat something." Malcolm got some leftover Thai salad out of the refrigerator. At least Jelani was real. All Malcolm's friends from college were still working out scales. One of them had actually referred to himself as "the recipient of a nationally recognized prize."

"Adulthood is riffing," Malcolm said aloud.

As he reheated some matzo ball soup Milla had made for his parents the previous night (she still wasn't that good at it), Jelani put on the Go-Betweens. Great. An Australian band.

Who was that freckle in a bikini to him now?

"You ever thought of the women you had before Theanra?" After all this time, Malcolm still wasn't sure whether Jelani's girlfriend had a "d" at the end of her name or not: was it Thean*dra* or, as he kept saying, Thean*ra*? He always slurred the end, just to be safe.

Jelani began talking about Italian twins he'd supposedly done in high school. "Milla reminds me of them sometimes, her big thighs."

Malcolm had heard Jelani on Milla before. He wasn't jealous, like some guys might be, but what about their friendship? Here Malcolm was, trying to share something important, and Jelani was off on his big thigh thing. He took advantage of Jelani's attempt to bite through a matzo ball and said, "Right, like me, in college, I did this semester abroad, and there was this Australian girl. Remember my Visions of Landra song? That was about her. She had these tits, they looked like they were fake, but they weren't." He wasn't doing her justice. "They were really ripe, like they could pop any minute. She was an, an explosive force, you know?"

Jelani shrugged and nodded, chewing.

"She could talk to anyone. She played the violin for this metal band, she was a great violinist, and her natural smell was, like, tan. Think there's a song in this? Or no?"

He almost hoped Jelani would say no, but he said, "Whatever."

Before Malcolm could get his hands on a pen, he knew how it would go, and yelled the words to Jelani: "It's only in the ocean, that it's ever truly night, and you tried to drown me, and I tried to fight."

"There is no try." Jelani said. Malcolm sometimes enjoyed Jelani's *Star Wars* references, but more often than not, they ruined the flow and the mood. They weren't Mathletes doing problem sets in some basement, they were funk musicians.

"Wait," Malcolm said. In the beautiful indigo ink of his father's pen, he wrote down what he'd just said. Perhaps he should be focusing on his poetry, forget this shallow music business.

What kind of life could he have had with Sandra? He saw her cowboy hat hanging off the doorknob, a wave arcing over his head. For what had he returned to the States? For college, which was useless to artists. There was Milla, and there was Izzy, and he cleaved unto them, sure, but with Sandra, it would have been a Blakean life. "What kind of boy you want today? To play?" Malcolm was trying to get Sandra's spontaneity across, but having to rhyme was ruining it. "Let's go wrestle. Outside. Let's go to the park." Milla and Izzy would be there, though.

"What's with wrong with you?" Jelani passed him the bong.

"Nothing's *wrong*," Malcolm said. "It's just I'm —" He'd expected to finish the sentence with the words, "still hungry," but "trapped" came out instead. What was that about?

He got up and began to pace before the windows, purposely stepping on the bottoms of the red velvet curtains. How had he ended up here, living with his parents and a child and a wife who was far from being the hottest woman he'd ever met? And another day was ending, and he still wasn't famous, he still wasn't anyone whose name the other Strausses would drop. How had this happened to the boy who'd played in a piano bar at the age of eighteen, hiked the bush alone at twenty? "I'm not blaming Izzy, he's just a baby, that's what they do, cry for like eons. It just feels so small here, you know?"

Jelani looked around the living room.

"Not spacewise. Internally. And our room is really small. It's like, am I going to just be a dad? That's what Milla acts like." Jelani took another drag. "Does Theandra ever pressure you?"

Jelani said what Malcolm knew he would say: He and Theandra were open, so it was different. To Malcolm, it seemed not only different, but also better. Open, by definition, was better than closed; even if you only listened to those two words, you'd know that.

"You know Milla, though," Malcolm said.

Jelani leaned back on the smoking sofa and gave Malcolm some excellent advice, really freeing his mind, so that at the end, Malcolm didn't know how to express his gratitude, could only endeavor to freestyle some riffs in the style of Prince.

Nadia Kalman

Osip

Only Osip was on hand to greet the Rehmans: Pratik's parents and grandmother, three tiny, sleepy, people, accompanied by strapping, suitcase-swinging, dentist cousins from Pennsylvania. Yana and Pratik were shouting upstairs, Katya was hammering in the basement, and Stalina was clanking in the kitchen.

The two Mrs. Rehmans stepped away from Osip's proffered hand. "You are a little like Orthodox Jewish ladies," he said, putting his hand in his pocket. He wanted them to know that he knew people like them, that they did not seem strange to him.

"I'm afraid they don't understand English," Mr. Rehman said.

Not having prepared an alternate topic, Osip continued his theme of unity, "Islam is in many ways close to Judaism. You have Moses, too, yes?"

"Indeed." Mr. Rehman said, smiling, but without attempting a translation.

Osip smiled. "Stalinatchka!"

Something in the kitchen crashed. Stalina emerged, with the fixed smile and crab walk of a game-show hostess. "Welcome to America," she said, sweeping her arm to encompass the living and dining rooms, for which she'd recently purchased gold slipcovers. "Make yourself at home. You know, in Jewish law, we say, 'Be good to strangers, because you were once stranger, and not only stranger — slave.'" She proffered a plate of shish kebobs.

Pratik's grandmother pointed at the skewers and spoke rapidly. "We are very tempted," Mr. Rehman said, and then asked whether he might ask whether the meat had been certified for Muslim consumption.

Stalina continued to hold out the plate, as if it were a baby they'd failed to admire. "But they are shish kebobs."

Osip excused himself to go get the children.

Upstairs, Yana was pacing her bedroom in a long, green, Indian-style dress. "You're the first generation," she said. "You want to be Westernized. Duh."

"Mr. Molochnik," Pratik said, "You have just met my parents, have you not?"

"Have you not?" Yana mimicked.

"Is it your impression, Mr. Molochnik, that they would be very excited to now have a strange American girl kiss their feet?"

Yana wrapped a tie-dyed scarf around her neck. "It's like I'm too Bengali for you."

"Bangladeshi," Pratik said.

"Not all the time, like my family's from Ukraine, but sometimes we say we're Russian, to make it simpler. I've heard you say 'Bengali.' You're just saying 'Bangladeshi' now to shut me out."

"Parents are here," Osip said. Something of the panic of the previous scene must have lingered in his voice, because the children immediately stepped into the hallway. Behind Yana's back, Osip raised his eyebrows at Pratik, to signify manly unity.

Katya had already come up from the basement, and was perched on the edge of the couch, unaware she was still holding a small screwdriver.

Pratik embraced his family. "Good stuff," his father said.

"In America," Stalina said, placing a hand on Mr. Rehman's arm, "we say, 'good evening,' not 'good stuff.'"

Yana cast her eyes down, perhaps in keeping with some other custom she'd read about, perhaps to get a preliminary look at the Rehmans' feet, shuffled forward, and introduced herself.

Pratik said, "Yana is very interested in Bangladeshi cooking."

"Is that so?" his father said, smiling.

"Yes, she made some egg —"

"Haloa," Yana said.

Katya leaned forward. "Yeah, for me and my, my friend Roman, and he said it was the best dessert he'd ever had, Russian, Georgian, American, any kind." She was acting as if Roman were some King Solomon of food. Worry fluttered in Osip's stomach.

The grandmother began to speak and point at the stairs. The other Rehmans frowned.

"What does she say?" Osip said.

"It's nothing." Mr. Rehman sat next to her. She spoke again.

"Come on," Osip said.

"She is merely asking how many floors your house possesses."

"Oh, oh," Stalina said, positioning herself in front of the grandmother. "Our house has three floors" — she held up three fingers — "many houses in America very *tall*" — and she stood on her tiptoes.

The grandmother spread the fingers of one hand and said something else. The dentist cousins smiled at each other.

"Does she has other questions about house?" Stalina said.

"No," Mr. Rehman said.

"What, then?"

He looked at the rug. "I'm not certain why she says this, but she wishes that I tell you she has five floors in her house, in Dhaka."

"That's right," Yana said.

"Speaking of houses," Osip said, "Maybe the Rehmans want to see rooms where they will stay."

"But —" one of the cousins, the prettier girl, began to say.

"They're not staying here, Mom," Yana said.

Stalina said, "What, a hotel? Stamford Marriott is very crude."

"I sent you an email," Yana said.

Stalina leaned closer to the Rehmans. "Yana and her emails. One day — save homeless, next day, globe is too warm. I say, it is good for homeless to be warm."

Yana sighed through her nose. "I wrote 'major' in the subject heading."

"They're staying with us, actually," the male cousin said.

Stalina stared at her handkerchief, as she often did in times of difficulty. "But, you know, Russia has a rich and sweet tradition of *gosti* — hospitality —"

Osip put his arm around Stalina. "Our house is not tall enough for grandmother." Stalina gave a false laugh. Why had he said that? After the Rehmans left, she'd wonder, aloud, for hours, whether the insufficient grandeur of their house was to blame.

"Speaking of culture," Yana said, dropped to her knees before the couch, and tried to take hold of Mrs. Rehman's brown-sandaled feet. Mrs. Rehman scurried her feet away in alarm, but Yana was faster, overtaking them as they sought refuge beneath the couch. The cousins stepped forward.

"It's a contact lens," Pratik said, in a voice quiet with despair.

"Oh, terrible luck," Mr. Rehman said, and quickly translated. Yana released Mrs. Rehman's feet.

"I'll help you." Pratik knelt beside Yana, his shoulder touching hers. Because they needed it, Osip silently gave his blessing.

Roman

When he let himself in, Aunt Alla was sitting at the kitchen table with a glass of iced water. He knew the lie she was about to tell. He didn't need to sit down.

"*She — a little too much, and went to a nameday and drank...*" *At least — in her sleep,*" Alla waited for him to say . . . what?

Alla took his sleeve. "*I'm remembering her in her bathing suit with the flowers, that summer before we left. Do you remember? In Feodosiya? Try to think of her like that, not —*"

Outside, he had some trouble seeing but learned not to look up. People got out of his way. He found himself at Caldor. Of course. A necklace made of two gold ropes wound around one another. He wouldn't wear it, he would sell it. He should have stolen jewelry from the beginning. He tried on the necklace. Oh, he was a real baller now, all right.

At the exit stood two officers, one white and fat and one black and thin. They told their walkie-talkies they had him. They took him to a small room in a Gulag movie and demanded his papers. The necklace fell to the table.

Like any Russian coward, Roman carried his passport and visa everywhere, wrapped in a handkerchief. He put the handkerchief on the table. It sprawled open. "All right, then," they said. It was one of his mother's handkerchiefs, cotton with some yellow embroidery. She'd bought it off an old woman on the street, who'd said "*Please, matyushki, so I can go home.*"

"You a student?" The black one looked like Tupac Shakur, who understood about mothers, and who was dead.

"Talk."

"Hello?"

"Maybe we better call Homeland. Maybe he wanted to sell the necklace for a bomb."

"Kid. We're just playing."

A door in the room opened onto the street. They lifted him outside. "Don't show your ass." The door closed into the stucco wall.

Yana

Just like a Bangladeshi girl, Yana put on all the jewelry she'd ever been given: a fake puzzle ring her parents had bought for her twelfth birthday, Navajo feather earrings, an amber necklace, a mood ring, gold bangles from Pratik's parents, friendship bracelets from camp.

She stood in front of the mirror and wrapped her sari, just like she had practiced, and it wasn't perfect, because before, her hands hadn't held these electrical surges, but she thought Pratik might already be downstairs, and she ran to meet him.

Instead, she almost crashed into Leonid, who stood at the bottom with one arm resting on the banister.

"Where's the dead man walking? Just kidding."

"The bride and groom are forbidden from seeing each other," Yana said, quoting directly from a website, and turned, and waded through the Russians, who pinched at her sari and made remarks, and the Bangladeshis, who inched away and stared, until she finally caught a glimpse of Pratik squeezed between cousins on the couch. The cousins faded into the party before Yana could say "*Kamon Acho.*"

Why hadn't they stayed? It must be a cultural tradition, she told herself. She cast her eyes down, as per custom, and said, "Shouldn't they be carrying us in on pillows or something?"

"Elephants."

"Monkeys." Yana took out her mirror (the bride and groom were not supposed to look at one another, except through a mirror; nor were they expected to speak, but she couldn't do everything). One of Pratik's eyebrows seemed to have found a home at his hairline. "You look crazed."

He squeezed her hand, which she'd had henna-ed in Queens.

"Do you like the pattern?" she said.

"Why not?" That was not a satisfying answer. She took another glance through the mirror. Why hadn't he brought a mirror of his own? Hadn't he wanted to see her?

Yana heard, inside her head, the voice of an actress who'd played Sojourner Truth in a movie she'd shown her class: "What you think you're getting up to now?" Women of genius said marriage was slavery. And yet, she had stuffed herself into silk. She had been a high school freshman only ten years ago. "You still think this a good idea, right?" Yana said.

"You cannot run in a sari." Pratik gave a laugh resembling that of Yana's borderline-autistic student. She had never before heard him laugh like that.

Stalina bore down on them. "Hello, young people. Pratik, it is an interesting smell your grandmother makes in kitchen. Yana, remove." She pointed at her ear.

"The tradition is — " Her mother held out her hand and Yana dumped the feathers into it.

Pratik's grandmother stepped out of the kitchen, carrying a large bowl of yellow paste. His mother, Moutushi, followed a few paces behind. "It's holud," Yana said, and the cousins by the dozens turned to stare. "It is, isn't it?"

Pratik's grandmother said something. He said, "Yes, it's her special recipe."

So, despite everything, they were going to do that amazingly tender ceremony (as it had been described online), whereby women applied a skin-softening turmeric paste to the bride's skin.

"The groom's not allowed to be present," she said.

"All right, all right." Pratik wandered outside.

The silk scratched against the gold lamé as Yana sat on the couch. She said, "This just means so much."

Moutushi handed her a Macy's shopping bag. Yana looked inside: a fish stared back. She closed the bag and smiled and nodded.

Stalina peered in. "Is this funny joke time?"

"It's a traditional gift. *God.*" Yana whispered.

"Did traditional God gift go six hours from Pennsylvania in a car?" Stalina took the bag to the kitchen.

Moutushi dipped her finger in the holud and gently spread it around Yana's eyebrows. It felt invigorating, like the acne remedies she had tried in vain all through high school. Well, a little more invigorating than that.

Her hand began to rise to her forehead, but Pratik's grandmother slapped it back down. The elder woman was right. So what if it felt as though Yana's skin was coming off? That was marriage, wasn't it? She was a marriage snake. Her new skin would grow in brown.

Katya

"We can leave, if you want," Katya said to Roman.

As they passed Stalina's figurine table, his fingers feathered out over it, as if he were testing the air, or deciding what to break. All he wanted, he said, was for her to write a list of the money he'd spent on her, because girlfriends cheat, but mothers are forever.

"Roma," she said, "Roma, slow down, I'll be forever."

He halted in front of the wine. "What, you want to marry me now?"

"Of course I'd marry you if you wanted."

He sat on the stairs. People ran around and past them. No one in their families stopped to talk. They were neither one of them a favorite.

Nadia Kalman

Pratik

Pratik's grandmother reached out her chicken-foot hand and pulled him into the Molochniks' cupboard.

"Your shoes, they are still on the landing," she said.

"Yes, dadi, I don't think Milla's sisters know all of our, our heritage." His father, and even his mother, laughed at this ritualized shoe-burgling. *"It's my fault for not telling them."*

She snuffled into her inhaler. *"All right, I forgive you, if will you now respect my suggestion?"*

From outside, Pratik heard Osip, sounding as though he were asking a question. *"Of course, dadi, as always,"* he said.

"Your cousin Keka. Look at me. Why are you marrying this Jew giant when Keka could be yours?"

Pratik's head reared back, knocking down a box of hot chocolate. The blonde girl on the package smiled up from the floor. *"Could we open the door a bit?"* he said.

"Keka is a good girl, a pretty girl. She'd be here now, but the American pigs at the airport said her name was the same as a terrorist's. But it was a boy terrorist they were looking for. Ha! They could have killed her."

"Dadi, you know I am to marry Yana," he said. *"But Keka is a wonderful girl, and I am rejoicing that she is still alive and not a terrorist."*

She pinched his hand. *"No one in our family wants that smelly Jewess."*

"If Yana's sisters steal my shoes, then may I still marry Yana?" Idiot. Had he really thought his family was coming to bless him? He should have taken Yana to an island somewhere, married her inside a hula hoop. *"Dadi, I believe Allah himself has fated this marriage."*

"Ha! You think Allah wants your Mongoloid brats?"

The pantry door swung open to reveal Katya and Roman, limbs intertwined.

"*Tell the monkey-pigs to run.*" Pratik ran from the pantry, from the house, and came to rest on the lawn, where it was too cold for anyone except a few angrily smoking uncles. He could go on. He could cross the street to the gas station and buy a newspaper.

Milla

"How's my skin now?" Yana said. At the combined suggestion of a dermatologist cousin of Pratik's, who'd (prematurely, in Yana's opinion) diagnosed an allergy, and their mother, she had finally agreed to rinse her face.

"Just a little pink," Milla said, patting Izzy's back.

"Sunburn pink or drunk pink?"

"Athletic pink," Milla said. Yana smiled, and winced, as a gang of boys, whooping and banging yellow spoons of holud against bowls, chased screeching girls from one end of the room to the other. Why didn't the girls escape outside?

Izzy gave a good burp as a boy named Igor ran past, chased by his Baba Mira, who was asking whether he wasn't ashamed before the bride.

When Milla had gotten married, everyone had said she looked so serene. No one would be saying that to Yana, she thought, as her sister bolted away, sari skirt clenched in two raised fists, to find their mother's bangles. Yet, underneath Yana's nerves, happiness buzzed and stung, and her sister threw what she had no idea was a movie star smile over her shoulder.

Would Yana really leave her here alone? Their mother still thought she could convince her not to go, during the few months Yana was to remain in the U.S., finishing her year of teaching, before joining Pratik in what he kept calling his motherland. Could Stalina do it? A few years ago, Milla would have had no doubt.

She hugged Izzy to her chest. He looked proud, as he often did after urinating. "Do you need a diaper change? I forgot the powder. I'm sorry. I did bring the cream." The garrulous baby in the book Katya had sent said, "I wuv to process language," but it was as difficult to speak to Izzy, especially in public, as it was to speak, at Malcolm's prompting, during sex.

Her Aunt Valentina threaded her way through the paths of

running boys. "*Diki ujac*," wild horror, she said, and then asked, like everyone else had, where Malcolm was. Milla explained that he had an important show.

"*Nu, he's an artist*," Valentina said, patting her purplish coiffure. "*You have to be like Nadezhda Mandelstam.*"

"*Horosho*," okay. Milla smoothed Izzy's hair.

"'*Horosho' is not enough.*"

Izzy — good boy — stirred and muttered. "I have to go change him," Milla said. Her Russian had run out.

"Maybe you will change — husband with me?"

Milla smiled and walked towards the stairs, past Katya making out with that Roman, past Bangladeshi girls dressed in blue saris, moving their hips in synchronicity and counting softly in English. Why couldn't she be one of those girls? She bumped into her mother outside the bathroom.

"*Moy Americanetz*," Stalina said to Izzy, and then to Milla, "*He, at least, inherited my cheekbones.*" Every member of the Molochnik and Strauss families thought Izzy resembled him or her, except for Milla's father, who thought he resembled Galich.

"He needs a change," Milla said, as her mother bore him away.

In preparation for the wedding, Stalina had redecorated the bathroom: a tiger dispensed paper towels, and fuchsia fur sprouted from the toilet seat, which Milla closed and sat upon. She dialed Julie's home number. She was in town, after all.

"Old married *baba*, how are you?" Julie sounded so enthusiastic. Milla's call was a wonderful surprise, which brightened the usual weekend dullness?

Milla told about her job. She was a full accountant now.

Julie said she was still at the old place, but not for long. "I am almost old married *baba*, like you."

Milla held the phone away from her ear. "Happy," she said.

"He is old boyfriend I was girlfriend to in high school. Now is under-minister for waste on farms."

The wedding would be in Poland; otherwise, Julie would have invited her. As Milla was forcing herself to ask whether there was a wedding website, or somewhere she could see photos, someone knocked on the door. "*Lyagushinka*," Baba Byata said, "*open up.*" She took the opportunity of Milla's silence to defy bourgeois proprieties, in English, no less, and ask whether she was "kaka."

Stalina

Stalina waved at Mr. Rehman from the top of the stairs and lifted up Izzy for him to see. He looked properly impressed. Truly, Mr. Rehman was quite a man. He'd loved that documentary on Entebbe she'd lent him.

The handkerchief interrupted her thoughts. *"Of course, our multifarious nation has always included some Asiatics, 'so many countries, so many customs,' it's all very diverting. However, the essential Russianness must remain. Where is the essential Russianness?"*

"I made vareniki." Stalina saw now, through jaded eyes and handkerchief, that what she had considered her greatest victory — an agreement to have the wedding here, rather than in the wilds of Pennsylvania — had been pyrrhic. Look at these girls, lip-synching into her Modernist dining room table, treating it the same as they would a bathroom mirror in a train station.

"The Eastern hordes are overrunning these nuptials."

"What could I do? It was the grandmother with her asthma. Anytime someone says no to her, she starts puffing."

As she descended the stairs, someone caught her by the arm — Edward Nudel, with his wife Ella. *"Guard your proudest adornment,"* the Soul said, and then added, unnecessarily, *"virtue."*

"Such a little punim, may I...?" Ella Nudel said, and held out her arms for Izzy. Babies loved Ella, Stalina remembered, as Izzy lolled open-mouthed on Ella's rest hotel of a bosom.

Edward was wholly uninterested in Izzy, as he had always been wholly uninterested in anyone without at least a master's degree in one of the physical sciences. With a certain air of obligation, he made the joke: *"Bangladesh just formed."*

Stalina completed it: *"Use baby oil and it'll go away."* It was remarkable how many of her friends and relatives had remembered this grizzled bit of Soviet humor. What else did they remember —

preschool praise songs to diversion dams? The favorite chocolates of long-dead district doctors?

Edward cleared his throat; he was usually only one joke away from his main point. *"Stalinatchka, I must take at least ninety seconds of your time."*

"Are you going to try to seduce me into your lab again?" She'd chosen the wrong word, provoking an odd look from Ella and a whispered rebuke from the handkerchief. If they only knew: in his old age, Edward had become so fragile it was frightening to kiss his cheek, let alone anything else.

Edward said, *"We are now fully equipped to conduct combinatorial chemistry at the highest levels, so you see, you have no choice but to join."*

"Edward thinks it's all very interesting," Ella said, rocking Izzy.

"What sorts of compounds...?" Stalina tried to sound casual.

"For shame," the handkerchief said. It had no right to interfere — it had stopped bothering to accompany her to the dull hospital lab long ago.

Ella said, "N*ow, my dears, my new friend and I go in search of zakuskis and tea,*" and bounced Izzy over to the buffet. Stalina couldn't help a huge smile as Edward described his new Cellomics ArrayScan. The difference between her current lab and Edward's was like the difference between cutting trees with handmade tools and cutting them on a tractor or with a chain saw or some such thing. She listened for almost an hour, stopping only when the handkerchief warned of her lord and protector's approach.

Osip

The rabbi and imam were gone; everyone had their shoes back; Izzinka was napping; Milla was crying; the Russians were drunk, the Americans more so: what better time for a toast? Osip stood, briefly lost his balance and grabbed the side of the cabinet. Stalina's figurines swayed, their yellows and navies and browns blurred together, it was beautiful — why couldn't Stalinatchka see the beauty?

"Wedding friends," he said. "I am losing daughter, but getting country. A small country, but, still, very nice." A few small smiles were his only response. He was trying, he wanted to say, he was trying to be funny about this awful plan.

"So we are very happy, and — we love you." The Russians applauded fervently, the Americans politely, the Bangladeshis warily. Yana and Pratik sat as they had since dinner, like electro-shock patients, with fingertips touching on the top of the table. Stalina asked Mr. Rehman to make a toast.

"I have prepared absolutely nothing." Mr. Rehman stood and walked to the head of the table. "Perhaps, instead, I could simply translate Mr. Molochnik's speech into Bengali?" but Stalina shook her head.

"Good luck," Osip said.

"Thank you, I will certainly need it." Mr. Rehman coughed and reddened.

"Yes, but you should say, 'To the devil!' That's how we say in Russian."

"We are speaking now English," Stalina said. Osip sat down.

Mr. Rehman said, "I will begin with a quotation from the Koran, if you do not mind."

"Of course we do not mind, we are open mind," Stalina said, crossing her arms.

"All right, then, the Koran tells us that humans do not choose whom we love. Rather, the Lord Allah chooses, and when we listen to him, he blesses us."

Now he translated into Bangladeshi, and even those guests who did not know the language looked upon him with respect. "As some of you know, my son Pratik has recently completed his dissertation on disaster preparation. Is not marriage itself a kind of disaster, in the very best sense of the word? Suddenly, another life is swept in to our shores, like silt in a flood."

"Yana now is silt?" Osip said to Stalina, in what was not quite a whisper. Why couldn't any of these groom-fathers simply say the bride was beautiful and sit down?

Mr. Rehman paused. "At first, we do not know what to do with this new gift. Sometimes, indeed, we rather wish the waters had never come, that our old life could continue apace."

5

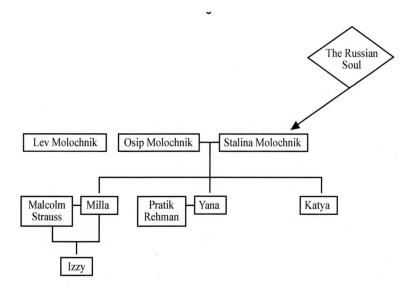

Lev

Osip said, why not have the leaf ceremony Labor Day weekend? Our parents were Soviet people, after all.

"Did you know my parents, winners of the Stalin medal?" he'd written, asking the readers of Russian-language newspapers with names idealistic (*The New Russian Word*), futuristic (*Contact*), Canadian (*The Canadian Russian-Language Newspaper*), imperialistic (*Our Texas*), and diffident (*By the Way*). He hadn't been sure whether or not to mention that they'd immediately given the medal to a Mongolian orphan, that he might exchange it for food. It was an unusual, and certainly memorable, deed — but our parents may have been too modest to tell anyone outside the family about it, so in the end, he'd left it out.

Someone had written back. Osya read aloud, "'*I knew a Solomon Molochnik in Kolyma, but he'd never been a captain. And —*'" Osip showed me a black-and-white photograph of some men, not in military regalia, standing in front of a hut. Our father was furthest to the right.

I said, "Don't you remember? He had much bigger ears than any of those men. Poor Russkie fogies, seeing a lost camp comrade in every newspaper ad."

"*Next year,*" Osip said, "*Maybe we can all travel to Mongolia and visit the hospital our parents saved.*"

"They tore it down," I said, bringing the tea to the table.

"*What, just like that?*"

"The Mongolians did so much damage it wasn't worth fixing."

Incompletely reassured, he joked, "*I wish those Mongols would come to Yankee Surgical.*"

I should have said something else, to tie together the sticks of that story. Osya would have pitched in, we could have raised that barn again.

He leaned forward. "*Will you speak over the leaf?*"

I told him, fine. Let him plan what he wants. Didn't I once plan to break our parents out of Kolyma in a helicopter? Didn't we brothers plan that if we ever got to the U.S., we would start a company together, become those monocle-wearing capitalists we'd only seen in cartoons?

Nadia Kalman

Milla

Milla saw the scribbled notes on their bedside table:

Isidor's Song

My father was made of cash
But you and I are built to last
Wanted to love her but didn't (repeat)
Now my son is the one I love
You will always be good enough

When Malcolm returned from rehearsal, she looked up from nursing Izzy and said, "You'd love to love me, baby?" She'd meant it as a joke, a musical, pointed joke, harkening back to that disco era song, pointing forward to their future, when they'd laugh about how she'd misunderstood what he'd written. She now realized she had been too ambitious with the joke.

"You looked at my song?" Malcolm said.

"It was right there." Izzy chewed on her nipple. When he was done, would her nipple be gone? Or would it stand proud, like a tattered flag after a battle? She wished she hadn't started this problem with Malcolm and that they were making nipple jokes instead.

He paced and his shadow, too large for the room, climbed up and down the pink walls. "You never come to the gigs. And your body — shouldn't you be weaning him by now? It's like it's some sponge of motherhood."

"I'm a sponge?"

"No, I didn't say that, I would never say you're a sponge, I'm not such a horrible guy, see? What I meant, what I meant was" — he slapped himself on the head and Izzy stirred and unlatched — "what I meant was, you don't see yourself as a, a sexual being anymore, you know?" Milla tried to reattach Izzy, which only woke him up further. "Like Jelani and Theandra, you know, they've been together longer than we have, and fine, they don't have kids, so that helps, but they have this sexual adventurousness that I think I could have, too. We could have. I mean, you had my son. Do you know how special that is?"

Izzy kicked Milla in the crook of her elbow, beginning his war dance. "Izz," she couldn't help almost shouting. Her right arm was covered in bruises. "Take him?"

"What — sure — what?"

"Can you sing to him or something?"

"Okay, in a sec, just let me finish. You wanted to know, so I'm telling you."

"He's going to start crying." Milla petted Izzy's warm, sweaty head. Once in ten times, this soothed him.

"Jelani said something, and even though I thought it was a good idea —" Izzy murmured. Malcolm turned to face the green mirror. "So I thought it was a good idea, but I didn't even want to ask you, and I think that's really kind of pathetic, that we can't even talk about something like this."

Izzy began to bawl. "I told you," Milla said.

Malcolm took him. "Do you hear yourself? Do you hear how vindictive you sound?" He began singing "Dock of the Bay" in his deepest voice. Izzy quieted.

A moment later, Jean crept in, in a lacey white nightgown, to suggest "Brother, Can You Spare a Dime," which had always gotten Malcolm to sleep.

Yana

The district director of social studies disliked Yana's boots, so she'd borrowed the lowest of her mother's absurd heels for work, and had gone straight to Central Park afterwards, skipping a war protest. Milla had been silent for the entire length of their walk to the reservoir. Yana wanted to tell her, "I don't play," like she'd heard another teacher say to his class.

Milla stopped before the railings. Izzy stared through the bars with an angry expression, like he was trying to scare someone straight. Finally, Milla said, "You know when you have a friend, but the friend gets really involved with stupid things, and then you have to let her go?"

"You mean like drugs, a gang?"

Milla sighed loudly through her nose. "I don't know anyone in a gang, I'm a married accountant with a child."

"Well, so-rry. You're being really confusing, I thought maybe this was about me leaving. Like, a sisterhood ritual, maybe we'd light bark on fire and throw it in the water."

"Are you crazy?"

"What? It's a Native American tradition." Yana wished she could remember which Native Americans — another chunk of her major lost.

Milla's eyes were watering. "Don't talk about leaving. I'm sorry, I can't —"

"Okay, okay," Yana said, patting her back, and making a goggle-eyed face at Izzy. She had wanted to explain to Milla why she was leaving sooner than planned. Their house had become unlivable: Katya and Roman sneaking around all the time, christening the bathroom and possibly Yana's own bed (a tiger-striped condom in the wastebasket by her desk); Roman's ghetto-speak, deeply offensive to someone who actually worked with children from what ignorant people called "the inner city"; Stalina and her daily commentary on

Bangladesh, always pertaining to the size either of the country or of its inhabitants.

Milla took a tube of purple mascara out of her coat pocket. "This reminded me of my friend, it's her favorite."

"What friend?" Yana said, as a unicyclist passed.

Milla shook her head, dropped the mascara into the wild, gray water, stared. "Where are the ripples? There are supposed to be ripples, where the fuck are the ripples?"

The sight of Milla in her working-mom flowered dress, hanging over the edge of the railing and cursing, frightened Yana. "Mascara's pretty heavy," she said. "Paraben." A couple of pretty Korean girls with cameras waited for the railing to become free. Izzy had fallen asleep, and she thought about poking him, so he would cry, so Milla would have to get down. She would give it one more minute, thirty more seconds....

She pulled at Milla's shoulders. "Come on. I have to get back."

"I just fucking hate her. She tried to fuck things up with Malcolm."

"What, she hit on him?" Some women had no respect. Pratik's boss in Bangladesh had been making him lunch. Yana narrowed her eyes at the Korean girls. "He didn't do anything?"

"Of course not. You know Malcolm."

"So, there was no problem, really. You have a great marriage." Telling Milla that usually calmed her down. "Should we start heading back?"

"You can go, if you want."

Yana couldn't bring herself to poke a child. She could, however, bring herself to remove a child's hat, before replacing it so that the wool covered one eye. Izzy awoke, complaining. "Give him his paci," Milla said.

"What's a paci?" It worked. Milla climbed down. "Jesus Christ."

"What? I'm fine." Milla shaded her face from sight as she fixed Izzy's hat.

"Milly —"

Again, her sister wouldn't let her talk. As they walked back through the darkening park, Milla told her that Malcolm played

Izzy songs on the piano, read aloud to her at night, called in the afternoons to see what kind of dinner she wanted to order. When she didn't want to face his parents, he brought food to their room.

Osip

It was five in the morning, cold, damp. Osip remembered being in the army, patrolling on mornings like this, only a thin uniform covering his skinny ribs. Some boys would purposely skip breakfast, in order to faint and, with luck, spend the rest of the day in the slightly warmer infirmary. Osip patted the sleeves of his puffy jacket.

Yana opened the door, wearing the long green dress she'd worn to meet Pratik's parents, and, over it, the yellow coat she'd had since high school. She really was leaving, then. After a short tug-of-war, she let him carry her suitcase down the steps.

He said, "You look a little like a plant in the dress."

"Sari."

Even though Osip remembered what the word meant, he said, "Sorry? You are one dressed like plant, I'm okay."

"Is this so I don't miss you?" She tuned the car radio to her liberal station, on which two girls and a rapper, a soft-spoken man who'd appeared a few times playing a by-the-books social worker on *The Commish*, compared the President to a rubber chicken. (Or a lover chicken? Incomprehensible, either way, but Yana laughed.)

They were still only a few blocks from home, and where, exactly, did Yana think she was going? She had decided, of her own volition, to go to a place where hundreds of thousands of girls her age had drowned. "Maybe you stay here after all? I can —" He would fry potatoes for their breakfast, hire an immigration lawyer for Pratik.

Without turning from the window, she said, "It won't be easy there, like it is here, but don't you think we've gotten too used to things being easy?"

It was the stupidest thing she had ever said. Osip was careful to keep his voice low. *"I never heard my Baba Rufa complain that life was too easy."*

"That's what I'm saying. Most of the world doesn't live like us, most of the world lives like Baba Rufa."

Osip stopped to let a fire truck pass. *"What was wrong with Baba Rufa's life? She provided for her family, she had her friends over to play cards. Her house was not floating away. When products came in, we had a line, a nice line, with people talking, not a riot."*

Yana seemed not to have heard. "All I'm saying is, most people don't have four computers in their house."

"Computers are for my work."

"Do you know what I read last year? Americans are like people in limousines driving through the slum. But someday, the people in the slum are going to crawl out of their shacks and turn our limo over and set it on fire." Where had she read that? What limo? He and Stalina had not been able to afford a dentist until 1987. Had Yana ever noticed how many silver teeth her mother wore? Did she think it was a gangster fashion? Yana said, "It's okay if you don't understand. This is my thing. Pratik's and my thing."

He tuned the radio to a traffic report. It was easier to drive when he was angry, although it may not have been easier for the other drivers, who shouted at him to pick a lane, etc.

A yellow van came dangerously close to their front windshield. Osip honked. "Look," Yana said, pointing to the Garfield doll suctioned to its back window. "A cat, crossing our path: we have to turn around."

Who'd known Yana was so superstitious? Stalina had taught her well. The luck rising in his chest, Osip began to make his way into the right lane.

"Dad. I was kidding. Didn't you hear anything I said before?"

She was silent the rest of the way, and he hummed Galich in order to sound happy. As he pulled onto the airport ramp, she said, "I already bought my ticket, I can't not go." A stupid reason. Osip was no materialist. He'd pay for her ticket, for ten tickets.

She scrambled out of the car. "Pop the trunk?" He wasn't going to let her hoist luggage. His stomach hurt with the effort of removing the bags. "I got it," Yana said. Osip held on to the handle of the largest suitcase — the dark green one that taken them to Grand Cayman. She wouldn't be able to wrest it away from him; he'd won a few more minutes.

In the end, like any determined criminal, she escaped. "See you later, alligator," he managed to say.

"Oh, because of the green?" Yana laughed: she was trying to make a nice memory for him.

She walked into a crowd of women dressed just like her, but half her size, so that she appeared, from the back, to be some kind of super Bangladeshi of the glorious future.

***

A few nights later, Osip lifted his wine glass. "*So, as they say, Yana's gone — let's drink to Yana.*" He didn't want any, himself. It shouldn't be, in this modern age, that husbands come like marauders to take daughters away: first Malcolm, then Pratik, and now this Roman had come to drink Osip's wine and have his way. As soon as everyone finished clinking, Roman stretched an aggressively muscled arm past Osip to fetch mushrooms for Katya.

Osip took a bite of his fish. Stalina liked people to know which ingredients she'd used; otherwise, what was the point? For example, when she cooked something in lemon, you knew.

"The fish is too dry, Roman?" Stalina said.

Roman put a giant portion on his fork, and began saying, "*Oh, no, it's very —*"

"No, you must to practice English!" Stalina said.

Roman took a gulp of wine. "Fish is banging." He banged a fist on the table and the glasses hopped. Stalina gave Osip a look. Before Roman had arrived tonight, she'd told Osip how unsuitable he was: he'd never finished college, besides which he was *mallo-culturni*, little-cultured, his mother was a *narcomanka* and he probably was one, too, and on top of all that, Stalina was almost positive she'd once seen him put five Daffy Duck watches in his pants at Caldor. It was fine for him and Katya to go to movies together, or ride bicycles, but now that Katya had invited him for dinner, the elder Molochniks needed to present a united front against seriousness.

Katya was happy, so there was that. Shaving her head had made her happy, dropping out of high school had made her happy, drinking and drugs had made her happy, getting a tattoo with a picture of a singer who'd killed himself had made her happy, and now Roman. "*Happiness,*" Baba Rufa used to say, fluttering her arthritic fingers, daring it to alight on her purple veins, her bruised knuckles.

"I got for you dishtowel," Roman said now, and pulled a neatly folded cloth from one of four front pockets on his fat man's jeans. Stalina held it up. Printed on the front was a pink kitten crawling out of a cookie jar, like a demonstration of a dirty kitchen in a hygienic comradeship filmstrip.

Stalina took a breath. "You find it at Caldor, maybe? You find it or you buy it?"

Roman gulped some more wine.

"You found also at Caldor many watches? You are a lover of duck?" Stalina's technique was terrible. She should have been friendlier, should have established date and time first.

"Mom," Katya said, and rubbed the back of Roman's neck. Roman shook her hand off. He asked in Russian whether Stalina was calling him a thief. He wanted to know, because he and his mother had been called many names, and he had names, too, for the Molochniks.

Katya said, "His mother just —" and Roman said, *"What about my mother? You want to talk about mothers?"* He started babbling that he knew Stalina was a liar, he'd seen some letter, she was a liar with Brezhnev. Stalina had been right; he was a drug addict.

Osip told Roman he was sorry about his mother, but it was no excuse. Osip himself had lost both his parents and — Roman walked out without having to be told.

Katya ran after Roman to the end of the driveway, in her socks, and wouldn't talk to them when she returned.

In their bedroom, Stalina stood in her blouse and pantyhose and aimed her blame at him. *"If we were in Boston, of course, she'd be so busy with —"*

"Enough," Osip said. *"You think I'd move to Boston and what? Take money from your former lover's wallet? You think I'm a* boy toy *for you?"* He went outside and sat in his car. He thought about asking Lev whether he could stay with him for the night. It was already eleven thirty-seven, and he had to get up at six.

Stalina

Fortified by half an hour's worth of a teen beach drama, Stalina stalked the house in search of Katya. She'd often, over the years, watched young people's programs before confrontations with her daughters, to make them think: "Is there anything on Earth my mother does not know?"

She found her in the kitchen, under the sink, practicing what she'd been learning in her class for women who wished they were men. Stalina got a colander and began peeling potatoes. "Roman is too sketchy for you."

Katya scooted out from under and sat up, her head cocked, her legs folded. She looked impossibly small in that position, a stunted child, but her mouth went crooked and mean when she said, "Excuse you?"

"*How can you stay with him, after he behaved so coarsely?*" Stalina said in chorus with the Soul.

That terrible voice: "*We've started on the path upon which hundreds of millions of people have already followed, and upon which all of humanity is fated to tread.*" Katya stood and ran from the room — crying? — but no, she returned with one of Osip's Sharpie markers and, tearing off a paper towel, wrote on it: "We're getting married. Me + Roman." The potatoes rolled into the sink. "*I must also congratulate our loyal ally, Romania, on its steadfast progress towards an economy that is truly economic.*"

"*Yes, I'm sure — many such good qualities,*" Stalina leaned against the sink, cold water seeping into her sleeve, and called, "Osya," but he was upstairs on the web, too distant to hear.

"*The weakening of any of the links in the world system of socialism directly affects all the socialist countries...*" Brezhnev justified the invasion of Czechoslovakia. Katya scribbled, "Can Roman move in here?"

"Katyenok, think: Who you are? Who he is?"

Nadia Kalman

"What? I don't understand your English."

So easily, Stalina had shut down the voice of her daughter's happiness. She stuttered out, "You are good girl from good family."

"Roman's a Russian Jew and a Chaikin." Katya picked up her wrench and tossed it from hand to hand.

"Tell her she was meant for finer things, a big beautiful wedding to an officer, with parasols and merry peasants, village dances, fountains of borscht and vodka," the handkerchief said.

"You will meet someone better," Stalina said. *"Do you see any of the mothers here trying to svatat' their daughters with Roman? Does that mean nothing to you?"*

"Um, it means he's not popular with the biddies?"

What was a biddy? Like a birdy? "It means he is thief and narcoman."

"He happens to be straight-edge."

Stalina didn't know this word, either. Television had failed her. *"Narcoman,* straight-edge...I'll tell you some words. *Porok — za porog.* Sin — get back from door."

"Sin? I'm an adult."

"What kind of adult, Katyenok? You live with mama and papa and have no job." Katya narrowed her eyes, but this was no time to be afraid of her own daughter. "What, you want me to say, move him here, give him master bedroom for black-market dealings? The son of *narcomanka —* "

"And whose daughter am I?"

Tears trembled at the edges of Stalina's eyes. She forbade them. *"Kak?* The daughter of intelligentsia. Even when we have no money, for food even for you, your father and I never steal."

"Maybe you should have, right? My lack of carrot juice was my whole real problem, right? Very interesting to give me that letter in Russian when you knew I couldn't read it. You got to confess, you got to feel like a good person, but you thought I'd never find out what you wrote."

The handkerchief said. *"Tell her you will go out to the fields and die of exposure if she says one more word."* Stalina could only stare at the wire basket by the window, which held only one onion, which was sprouting.

Katya said, "It doesn't matter, because I did read it. Roman translated. Nice job, Mom, letting me think all along I was crazy, all along it was you and your whoring ass."

The handkerchief said, *"Tell her you never expected to hear such curses from your angelic, soft-spoken daughter."*

"I never expected to hear such curses from my angelic, soft-spoken daughter."

"Soft-spoken? I was just scared to talk, my whole life —"

Osip, carrying his oatmeal bowl, pushed open the door. "Katyenok? *Nu, what is this?"* Wide-eyed, he patted her back.

Theandra

Theandra had been Southern when she met Jelani, she'd never listened to any non-mainstream music, taken any drugs, or had a colonic. Listening to him recount these early deprivations, she wished she could go off somewhere and sketch, but she'd have to wait until tomorrow, when the Strausses would finally leave.

Jelani came to one of his punch lines, "I said, 'You dress like a les-bi-an.'" Theandra glared at Milla Strauss, who giggled with her hand to her mouth. Messing around with white couples was annoying from beginning to end. The women were so eager to eat her out, as if to say, "Isn't this much nicer than when we were all lynching each other?"

After fifteen more minutes of giggling, she took Milla Strauss' hand and led her to the bedroom. For a few minutes, she would be the expert. Little as she might know about acid jazz or accounting, she knew much more than this or that bi-weekly bi-curiosity about what would happen next.

This one kissed her as soon as they got into the bedroom, using her tongue and pushing back Theandra's jacket, which wasn't how it was supposed to happen. "Hey," Theandra said. She'd made that jacket herself, and anyway, they were both supposed to get undressed, turn on some music, and massage each other until the boys were ready.

"Sorry," Milla Strauss said, but didn't stop. Probably congratulating herself on her jungle passion.

"Hold up here." Theandra backed away, checked the jacket, which seemed fine, and put it on the hanger. "There's plenty of time for that. See —"

Milla Strauss drew Theandra's lips inside her own. "Wait," Theandra mouthed, pulling Milla's acrylic accountant sweater from her shoulders. "Just. Hold. Up."

A few minutes passed. As a child, Theandra had watched

afternoon movies with her grandmother, and now she saw, not what was happening, but how those movies might have hinted at it: oil pouring from a glass tumbler, a champagne bottle uncorking.

At first, she didn't recognize Jelani's voice. "Looks like they've started without us," he said, sounding not quite as pleased as one might expect. "All right, then, man, who you want first?"

"Uh…" Malcolm Strauss stammered at this unexpected etiquette dilemma. "They're both looking good to me right now, I guess."

Milla Strauss dropped her head back onto the bed. Theandra went back to what she had been doing.

"See, what we have here," Jelani said quickly, "Sometimes, it's more like a freaky peep-show type of situation."

The men leaned against the wall. The men cracked some jokes. Milla Strauss held Theandra's hands in hers and kissed down the nape of her neck.

Milla

Neither of Malcolm's parents could operate their DVD projector, so Malcolm usually had to get the film started, and then stayed behind to watch it with them in the study. Tonight, Izzy was calm, so Milla had been able to bring him in to watch, too.

The brick-colored walls made the room seem even smaller. On the small marble table that partially blocked their view sat a framed photograph from Milla and Malcolm's wedding, in which Milla, looking particularly lumpy-cheeked, was embracing or accosting Malcolm from behind.

Jean paused *Jezebel* at the ballroom scene and pointed the remote control at Malcolm. "Are you like Pres?"

"I don't know," Malcolm said, flipping forward another page in his old biology textbook. (He was considering applying to a Ph.D. program.) Milla leaned against his arm. Malcolm would never publicly humiliate her like Pres had Julie. No, if Milla wore something slutty, like Julie's dress, he would be proud.

"Don't you think he's an asshole?" Jean said.

"Language," Bobby said from the high-backed chair he'd placed within a nose of the screen, waving his hand in the direction of Izzy, who sat in Jean's small, upright lap, clutching at her beige skirt.

"Oh, he has no clue," she said, rocking her pointy knees back and forth.

"Freeze," Izzy said. He had learned it from watching television with Milla's father.

"You're so demanding." Jean stilled her knees and re-started the movie, only to stop it a minute later, to tell them about her new client, a Broadway actor suing for paternity rights, who refused to believe Jean was a grandmother. "Isn't that ridiculous?"

Bobby said she still looked like a coed. Jean waved her free hand, as she did whenever anyone complimented her.

Izzy said, "Abc, abc, abc."

"Does he know the alphabet yet?" Jean said.

"He said 'asbestos'," said Bobby, who was working on an asbestos case.

Malcolm smiled. See how happy he was now: all he'd wanted was to try new things, things that were fun for her, too. It was all right that Milla thought about Theandra once in a while, wasn't it? Yes.

Jean paused the film again. "I would have slapped him harder."

Malcolm said, "Stop wasting my time."

Katya

Roman and Katya took the bus downtown, past all the stores that had sprung up around the Swiss bank, through streets filled with apartment buildings rising like totems between aluminum-sided houses. She'd told her mother she was leaving, but she hadn't told her father, because he was refusing to speak to her. "I'm glad I'm getting out of there," she said, and took Roman's hand. He smiled slightly, no dimples, but still, a smile.

Yana chose that moment to call and ask whether she was sure about "the whole marriage caboodle." Katya had to take one step away from Roman so he wouldn't hear, which, of course, made him suspicious. Yana yammered on about how she herself, who was three important years older than Katya, had been very nervous when she'd gotten married, and her marriage had been to someone she'd known for years, and she'd been right to be nervous. "I've known Roman for years," Katya wanted to say, but she didn't want him to hear his name. Thankfully, the connection broke.

As they carried their bags past a calligraphied sign, "Augustine Manor: *Semper*," Roman explained in a whisper that somehow, using "hustler's tricks," his friend Chino had gotten a subsidized apartment there, and offered to share. Katya hadn't known they would be living with anyone.

Chino was a blonde guy who looked as if he should have been coaching a sailing team, but instead was watching a cartoon squirrel spray machine-gun fire through a forest.

"We can pull out couch to sleep here," Roman said, pushing their bags against the wall. "Queen-sized bed."

It was shaky, so Katya borrowed Roman's screwdriver and set to work. "I need you to watch, make sure I'm doing this right," she said, but Roman looked mostly at the television. Chino told Roman that he'd met with an army recruiter, that he was going to be a civil affairs officer in Germany, because he was smooth and German girls were crazy.

Asking Roman whether he felt okay would set him off, and of course he was okay, look at him. She kissed him ("Where's mine?" Chino said.) and left to meet Milla in the mall.

Milla cried the entire time about their father not letting her go to Katya's wedding. "I'll buy you a dress, at least," she kept saying, and trying to steer her towards Saks. Katya found something okay, and cheap, at The Limited. As Katya put her on the train, Milla tried to explain something about marriage to her, that if Roman wanted to — she should —

When Katya returned to the room, Roman was alone, sitting on the floor, a glass of beer in his hand, his eyes half-closed. She told herself again that, if there was ever an occasion to relax straight-edge rules, it was the death of a parent. It was just a beer. She put her arms around him, and he let her. He was getting better.

The air smelled burnt. She tried not to ask, got through almost an entire talk show about parenting an overweight adult child. "Does Chino smoke up?"

"Who?"

How dumb, to bring up something trivial like that. So what if Chino did? It didn't mean Roman would. "It's just really sad," she said, "your mother…" Brigitte, her friend from carpentry class, had said she should try to get Roman to talk.

"For Chaikins, yes. *Who'll be the family blyad'?*"

"*What's that word —*"

He waved the question away. "*You're not the lord of this house.*"

A few minutes later, he sniffed the air, and leaped to his feet, and tried to run out of the apartment, crying when she blocked the door. "*Why did you bring the bomb, why? You know I can't hit a girl.*"

He only calmed down when she promised to leave, and he wouldn't let her take her keys. She sat against the outside of the door. Little kids came from a nearby apartment and tried to sell her candy.

Stalina

Osip couldn't tell Stalina what to do, and she didn't have to tell him where she was going. He was sulking in front of a raid on a prostitution ring on television, and didn't turn around to say goodbye or notice she was wearing her spangled blazer.

The handkerchief talked of *yet another betrayal, how long would her lord continue to tolerate*, and so on. She drove to the address an all-too-pleased Alla Chaikin had given her. Alla Chaikin had blurted out that she was so relieved Roman was leaving her house, "*becoming independent, I mean, and marrying such a nice, intelligentnaya girl,*" that she and Arkady would pay for the entire wedding themselves. Stalina had made only token protests, uncomfortable as that was, because Osip would have noticed if she'd paid.

She pulled up to a Lutheran church. "You are welcome," two sweatshirted ladies inside the front door said, and sent her to the basement. If Katya and Roman were not inside, then it could mean that they were still waiting in line at the courthouse (a rabbi was too much *tsuris*, Alla had said), or it could mean they had changed their minds.

Stalina opened the door and saw the children immediately, because there were only about thirty people in the hall. Katya was wearing a terrible fringed cowlady dress and clinging to Roman's arm. "*She has staked her all on this Queen of Spades,*" the handkerchief said.

She hugged Katya, who made a crack about her father's silent treatment, and forced a hug from Roman, whose unwashed neck she could smell. They were married, that was it. She was going to make the best of it, as soon as she'd made sure.

"Yeah, Mom, we're really married, you can go to the corner and cry now," Katya said.

Banished, she prepared for the onslaught of Alla. However,

Alla and Arkady were busy talking to the other guests, all Russians, screeching and shouting about someone's pool party. Stalina knew some of the other people's faces, she'd seen them at Alla's parties, or when Osip dragged her to see some former singer from the former country performing at the JCC.

It smelled of coffee. Someone had left the door to the men's room open.

Stalina was not materialistic. She and Osip had had a very plain wedding. As long as the children were happy, what need had they of Jean-style champagne flutes, flowers, and music? Alla had ordered from the Russian deli, and the guests had clearly enjoyed the *salat olivier* and bagels: the plastic container had been scraped almost clean, the basket was empty but for half a yellow disk.

Alla finally approached, and said, "*Poor girl, you don't know anyone here but us.*" Was Stalina imagining her slightly vindictive tone? It was true that she and Osya had avoided Stamford's *Russkaya companiya*. They'd wanted American friends, straight-thinking, normal, easy people, only, the Americans hadn't wanted them. "*I can introduce you...*" Alla said, with too much pity in her voice for Stalina to be able to accept.

And where were Katya and Roman's friends? There was only one young man, blonde, in a camouflage jacket, passing a wine bottle back and forth with Roman. Everyone else was of her and Alla's age, they were Alla's friends, of course. It was not a fair wedding.

Someone plugged in a boom box, and when the first notes played, the guests shouted along, "Ai yai yai yai yai…"

Roman and Katya had vanished. The blonde young man was drinking alone. She pulled Alla's fleshy silk back away from the singing circle. "Where are the children?"

Merriment left Alla's face and it was all vertical lines. "*Do you know, Stalinatchka, Roman has never offered me a single word of condolence for my sister? The young are so selfish, aren't they? Not Leonid, of course, but we had a chance with him, we had him since birth.*"

Stalina drove in circles until she came to a gazebo that sat on a patch of land opposite a suite of dentists' offices. Inside were two figures, one flashing white in the darkening air. She parked her car in a traffic lane — who was around to stop her? The handkerchief

Nadia Kalman

had gone silent. Mosquitoes and fireflies hurtled in her path. At the same moment she knew that it was Katya, pulling on Roman's arm, Katya saw her, shook her head, waved at her to leave. For some reason, which Stalina regretted even as she opened her car door, she obeyed.

Milla

She came home from work to find Malcolm doing laundry, a red bandana wrapped around his forehead. He'd ordered in Japanese food, her favorite, which they couldn't really afford, but Milla was happy anyway: not everyone's husband would do that. Izzy was asleep in their room, so deeply asleep Milla had to watch for a moment to make sure his stomach was moving. It was, of course. She had to stop being such a worrier.

"It's weird, isn't it?" she said as they began to eat, "your parents going away?"

"Huh?" Malcolm was distracted, even for him. A grain of rice was stuck in the cleft on his chin.

"Just, your mom's always saying she never takes vacations."

"I told them we needed some time."

Milla pinched the grain off of him. "That's nice."

"Not just time, time to talk." He piled beef teriyaki on his plate, but instead of eating it, reached across the table and put his hand on her shoulder. She flinched for some reason. He said, "This has nothing to do with you. It's my fault, okay?"

"What?" She grabbed a fistful of edamame.

"Look, it's not fun enough." He got up and started pacing. "I don't mean it's not fun enough. I mean maybe not life-affirming enough. Or —"

"Quiet. Don't wake him." She felt the individual grains of miso, like spores of a fungus, inside her mouth. The gold-edged mirrors reflected and refracted her stupid pink suit jacket.

"He's fine. And I invite you to gigs, but you hardly ever come, and you don't like parties. And it's okay. It's great that you want to stay home with Izz and watch TV and shop online and eat leftovers. Somewhere out there" — that was line from a movie, wasn't it? Sung by a ragged mouse? "Somewhere out there, there's a guy for you, who likes those things. But I like to go out into the world and just explore, go to new countries, surf, meet people, have real conversations, you know? And there are songs I need to write, and I can't write them with —"

"You'll wake him."

"He's fine. I just gave him a little cough syrup."

"You *what*?" She ran to the crib and shook Izzy awake. "Are you okay? Does your tummy hurt? Do you want your bottle?"

Izzy started to cry. Tears leaked from Milla's copycat eyes.

Malcolm said, "It was just a few drops, man. My mom did it to me all the time when I was little."

"He could be brain-damaged." She started shaking.

"No way. Iz-man, what comes after one?"

He gulped. "Two." He poked Milla in the eye with two fingers. She tested Izzy's knowledge of their names, colors, objects. Malcolm eventually sat on the bed.

"Ready to get back to sleep, bud?" Milla said.

"No way." Izzy kicked her in the stomach, and it was too much all of a sudden.

"You want your movie?" she was barely able to say. Izzy was in love with a Hebrew language video, featuring impossibly young, busty mothers and their compliant children. He nodded.

"Turn it on. Please," she said to Malcolm, who'd wandered into the study after them. He knew the movie without asking. Those things were important in a marriage. The children spun around a blue and white parachute. Izzy sat on top of the back of the couch, which she usually didn't allow. She held on to his legs. "Maybe we can make it more fun," she said.

"I doubt it," Malcolm said, as if he were discussing the prospects of an inferior band.

"But you're my rock." Why had she said that? It wasn't true.

Malcolm said, "My parents are totally fine with having you stay for a while, so you don't have to worry about that." He crouched down in front of them, blocking the screen, and Izzy pushed at his shoulder.

"Can you move?" Milla said. Izzy climbed down and stepped on her thigh. "Ow." She pulled him onto her lap.

"Jean specifically wanted me to tell you to stay here as long as you want."

"Move," Izzy said, kicking Malcolm off balance.

Malcolm sat down hard on the floor, said "Owsers" with a small smile.

"You told them?" Milla said. The children made sandcastles in double time.

"Jean wanted me to tell you, she's been showing Izzy's photos to everyone in Cabo, and they're really impressed. People think he must be four or five, he's so big."

"She's not allowed." Izzy pushed at her cheek.

"What?" Malcolm crouched closer.

"It's unsafe to — she's not allowed. Tell her."

Malcolm raised a palm, "Let's calm —"

"I want you to tell her."

Malcolm shrugged. "All right." She had some temporary power. What else might she ask of him?

"We'll move out tomorrow." Izzy squirmed from her lap and threw himself on the floor.

Malcolm leaned back on his heels. "That's — soon." The children clambered aboard a hot-air balloon.

"What, you thought I'd hang around? Stay in your mother's maid's room?"

He leaned back. "You don't have to get so — "

"We should hug. I think." she said.

"Sure, I just didn't hug you before because I felt so weird. Come on, family hug," Malcolm said, and opened his arms and waited.

6

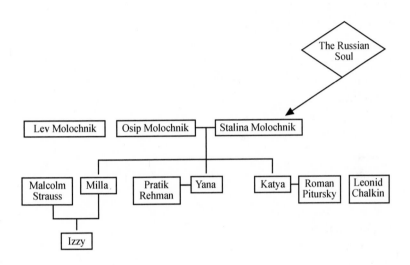

Osip

Osip had never driven a truck before, which had concerned the man at the rental company not at all. The man got paid either way so perhaps he didn't care. But Osip would be driving home with his daughter and his grandson, and he noticed with annoyance that his hand shook on the gearshift.

When he was eighteen years old, Osip had fallen fourteen feet onto a parquet floor. He had not been drunk or hooliganning. He had merely been following his colonel's order to put a new bulb in his Black Forest "war trophy" chandelier, and when he began swaying, had known not to reach out and grab the fragile glass. And for this, the floor sprang up at him?

Now, he felt a similar anger. For the sake of his so-called music, Malcolm would desert a girl like Milla Molochnik? Osip would hack Malcolm's web site, delete all those songs through which they'd had to sit: "So hard to juggle / My political struggle." What kind of struggle could it be when no one would ever be bothered to jail him?

He popped in a Galich tape. "Hussar's Song" began, and he blasted the martial chorus, muted the ironical verses.

Stalina called and Osip couldn't resist saying, "Don't worry about Malcolm. I take care of him."

"'Take care': *what, my dear friend, is that supposed to mean?*"

"*We will have a masculine conversation, that's all.*"

Stalina sighed, not in the manner of a maiden seeing her soldier off to war. "*He has thirty years on you, and plenty of free time to work out besides.*"

"*And I have my time in the Russian army.*"

"*Oh, so the two of you will be inspecting speedometers together?*"

"*You understand nothing. This is between me and him, your*

female jokes are stupid in such situations."

She was saying something about Malcolm's parents being lawyers when Osip hung up. This was serious business.

Malcolm

Malcolm was unspeakably relieved to hear the elevator stop outside his door, to hear suitcases roll close, to hear his mother trying to jam the key into the lock. He sat on the couch, in the same clothes he'd been wearing when he told Milla, the same clothes he'd been sleeping in, too, a Multicult tee shirt, his bandanna, stained jeans, and when he'd gone to the record store to avoid Milla's dad, a cute girl had fled the Funk section at his approach. Too tired to open the door, he listened to the key jam again, and to his mother: "Bobby? Did you ever talk to Carlos about the lock? Bobby?" and then his father got the door open.

His mother kissed him. His father said, "There's a certain musk," and fetched three glasses of water.

"It's so empty. Isn't it so empty?" his mother said, standing in the middle of the carpet in her stocking feet, holding the glass in both hands, like a child.

"Sit down, Jean," his father said.

"How do you feel? Did she really leave just like that? When are we going to see Izzy again? I thought she'd fight for the marriage. I guess she doesn't want to be married either, huh? What do you think?" She had double bags under her eyes.

"Sit down, Jean."

"How was it?" Malcolm said. His voice sounded as though he'd just woken up. He took a sip of water.

Jean said, "The hotel: what a laugh. We switched rooms four times. When are we seeing Izzy again? Nothing's final yet, is it?"

He knew he shouldn't say it, but he'd spoken to no one for four days. "It was surprising, how fast — I thought we'd talk more."

"Well, what do you expect? A woman scorned, she doesn't want to talk, right, Bobby?" She'd used Malcolm's words against him again, but he couldn't feel angry and didn't want to leave the room.

"I don't know," his father said to the ottoman.

"You don't *know*?"

"Sit down, Jean."

She sat on the edge of the piano bench. "Have you been pouring everything into your music? That's why you split up, isn't it, so you could be a rock star? Have you written loads of new songs?"

He had written only one, and it was probably crap. He confessed to it.

She sprang up. "Play it for us. Shouldn't he play it for us?"

He was grateful to have a reason to stand. He was grateful not to be facing his father. He was grateful for the cold, clean keys. He was grateful, almost to the point of tears, that his mother had asked.

Milla

Milla awoke face-down on a rough, bleach-smelling pillow: Stamford. Izzy. Where? "Izzy!"

"*Like a fishwife,*" her mother said, entering her room with a tray. "*He is sleeping very nicely in our room, like yesterday and the day before.*"

Milla tore out of bed and down the hall. It appeared that her mother had been telling the truth.

Before Milla had managed to climb back beneath her blanket, Stalina barked, "Kasha," and lifted a lid off a dish. The smell of old shoes steamed out at her. Her mother had forgotten — of course — that Milla was the daughter who hated kasha. Milla gave so little trouble, Milla had such an easy nature, Milla would forgive, Milla wouldn't mind. If Stalina cared to know, which she clearly didn't, Milla would have given anything for one of Malcolm's omelets. She'd never eat another omelet.

"Don't you have work?" she said. If her mother only left, she could call Malcolm again. She'd dreamed about another way he had mistreated her: he had never once considered her worthy of a conversation about literature. She'd heard him talk about Saul Bellow to his friends, but never to her. Well, he'd talk about Saul Bellow today, even if she had to wake him, which she would. (Yana had said, "Or, you could just write your feelings in a letter? You wouldn't have to mail the letter, necessarily, even." Milla had explained that an unsent letter wouldn't get her an apology. Perhaps it had merely been a bad connection, but Milla had been surprised by the wimpy, appeasing tone of Yana's advice.)

Stalina sat on the edge of her bed. "I have twenty minutes. You will tell me all your feelings of rejection and loss. Is normal." Her mother gave her the sticky, hot dish, and a brisk nod.

Milla said nothing.

"Now, nineteen minutes."

"Are you a psycho?" Milla said, knowing how nasty and adolescent her voice sounded, not that it had sounded that way when she'd actually been an adolescent, oh no, how could it have, between work and school, her grim youth portioned out in hunched shoulders and paper cuts.

Her mother put her hands on her hips and smiled an understanding smile. "It is like making pee, this sharing, yes?"

Milla said, "This is the most hurtful, the most stupid idea —"

"Ah-ah." Her mother shook her finger, but did not seem at all offended. "*Eggs do not teach the hen,* we will do this until you feel super-better."

"Super-better, what the —" not even Yana had been able to curse in front of their mother — "fuckety fuck fuck!" She threw the burning dish across the room: a summer storm of kasha, swift and fierce. When she looked back at her mother, Milla knew she wore an expression almost feral. She yanked off her wedding ring. It fell with a plink. She looked for other things to throw. The alarm clock: she'd never need it again, she'd never go back to work, she'd been driven mad. Her mother jumped out its way.

"*Millatchka, you'll wake the child, be careful,*" her mother said, reaching out a hand to her, but not stepping forward. Out of fear?

"*Be careful?* Are you fucking kidding me?" she said. This called for her to make some momentous statement, but, she didn't know whether she had been too careful or its opposite in marrying Malcolm. She threw her bedroom slippers at Stalina. They hit her knees. They were soft, they couldn't have hurt much, but her mother backed out the door.

Jean

There were few people Jean Strauss loved more than her lovely Greek secretary Helice. Just like that saying about how women should be lambs in — where? — she couldn't remember — and tigers in the bedroom, Helice was a lamb inside Jean's office and a tiger in the reception area. She screened everyone, even Bobby.

Which was why Jean was shocked to see Stalina running through her office door on her chunky legs.

"Oh — hi!" Jean said. "What are you doing here? Did you take the awful train?" She tried to peer past her for Helice.

"For a mad dog, seven *versts* is not out of way," Stalina said, slamming the door shut.

"Huh." Jean picked up a book to show she was busy, but unfortunately, the book was the biography of Betty Grable she'd been reading at lunch. She covered Betty's legs with her palm.

"Are you proud?" Stalina said. Her fist was clenched, surely she wasn't about to — but no, there was something in it, a tissue or something.

"I beg your pardon?"

Stalina leaned into her, so that they were practically nose-to-nose, Bugs Bunny and, who was that ugly man with the big nose? Him, that was who Stalina resembled. "How's Milla? And Izzy?" Jean said.

"Mee-la! You should say her name Mee-la! All these years I never correct!"

Jean backed up — fine, yes, showing weakness — and braced herself on her desk. "Look, they got married very young. When a couple has a baby, their relationship changes. I can't tell you how many —"

"I give you young, fresh, beautiful girl, bloom in innocence."

"Well, I'm pretty sure they were sleeping together before the wedding," Jean said. "Not that there's anything wrong with that, I'm no prude —"

"Now is like old *baba*. What your son the big prince do to my Milla?" Stalina opened her fist and took out a beautifully detailed lace handkerchief, with which she wiped her eyes. Was it from Provence? Jean wanted to ask.

Stalina said, "You're bitch," pronouncing the word like *beach*. It was laughable. The door slammed: who was this woman, a teenager?

Jean sank into her desk chair, which was new and stiff, and did not give. Should she have chosen the calfskin upholstery? (It had seemed cruel at the time; she'd remembered that she and Malcolm never ate veal.) She punched the arm. Where had Helice been?

"Someday, he'll come along, the man I love," Jean sang under her breath. It was comforting to hear her own voice, not so age-ravaged yet.

Nadia Kalman

Milla

Jean's secretary called to say that Jean would be in Stamford that afternoon. To say, not to ask. Milla wondered whether she was in trouble for those phone calls to Malcolm. She'd almost stopped making them, but she wasn't about to cease and desist entirely. If Malcolm didn't want to be called, he should have been a better husband. That was what she would say to Jean.

She wasn't going to put on any makeup, not for Jean. She wasn't going change Izzy into an unstained shirt, either. Three minutes before Jean was due to arrive, she did both, and then tried to read, but couldn't help scanning the window for the Mercedes.

Forty minutes later, a different kind of car, dark green, pulled in the driveway. "It's a Renault," Jean said from the driver's seat, strapping her high heels back on, "Isn't it sporty? Or maybe it's too young for me."

Izzy hugged her skinny calf as she stepped out of the car. Jean ran her fingers through his hair and dug into a paper bag. "Doesn't this look delicious?" She presented him with a jar of mashed peas in a brand Milla didn't recognize.

"He's a little old —" Milla said, as Izzy grabbed the jar and rolled on the grass with it.

"It's by special appointment to the Queen." Jean tried to crouch down, but her narrow skirt prevented her. "Oh, well, it's only us." She hiked it up to the bottom of the control top of her pantyhose, and balanced with one hand on the grass. "There's something for you, too, Milla."

"Great." What would it be this time — an umbrella emblazoned with the logo of a cosmetics company (Hanukkah)? The free digital camera that came with the purchase of Malcolm's computer (birthday)? *Last Tango in Paris* (anniversary)? What came free with ostentatious baby food?

Jean held up a velvet box. As Milla bent to take it, Jean looked at her hand and said, "Oh — you're not —"

Turning away slightly, Milla opened the box. Inside was a necklace with a small green stone, cut into a multi-sided sphere.

"Emeralds are the right month, right? Or no?"

"Thank you," Milla said. Her voice sounded as if it came from a cardboard tube.

"Oh, well. I still have the receipt." Izzy tore fistfuls of grass and rained them over himself. Was this necklace a ransom for Malcolm? Would this be the last time she saw Jean? "Are there ticks?" Jean said, "Should we go inside? Do you have money?"

"What?" Milla tried to draw Izzy towards her, but he was staring like Narcissus at the colors reflected in Jean's shiny pantyhose.

"Malcolm can't be sending you much."

They thought she was some pathetic immigrant, trying to get her hands — her *paws* — on their money.

Jean said, "You don't need to hide it from me. I'm a family lawyer, it's like being a doctor. Are you getting an apartment? You're not planning to live here forever?"

"I'll let you two play." Izzy and Jean stared as Milla went into the house, but they didn't notice her looking out the living room window, past the burning azaleas that always bloomed before her birthday. Jean led Izzy by the hand around the small perimeter of the lawn. They pointed at cars — two true Americans. Jean looked more natural with Izzy than Milla ever had.

Stalina

Lev said he'd gone by the apartment where Katya and Roman were staying, but no one had answered the door. When would he try again? Stalina said.

He didn't know, what was Stalina expecting him to do? He and Katya had barely seen each other over the past few years. He had a headache.

Fine. Stalina hung up. What use was Lev to his family, or to himself? "*Unkind*," the handkerchief said. Stalina frowned into the backyard, where Osip was trying to teach Izzy to box, or perhaps only to hop. She'd gotten Katya off drugs, hadn't she? "*And then lost her to the seductions of a cavalier*," the handkerchief said. She'd gotten Milla out of bed, mostly.

A few hours later, she called Lev back and said, "*When you talked about Perm in your lectures, you were happy, handsome and normal, yes? Now, you don't talk about Perm, and you can't even go outside to get your hair cut. Meals on Wheels, like an invalid. Shameful, no?*" Had she gone too far? "*Isn't it better to be happy, and handsome, and eat in restaurants?*" She fiddled with her gypsy figurine. How free and brave the gypsy looked. "*I have helped my girls with 'talking-it-out,' and now I will help you, and we will celebrate at Salvatore's.*" Salvatore's was an Italian and lobster restaurant on the north side of town, where Lev had once spoken on behalf of Ethiopian Jewry.

"*I still have that headache.*"

"*You know why you have headaches? I think I know. You talk about a bad smell.*"

"No, I don't."

She didn't let his switch to English distract her. "*Does it smell like the Isolator? That's what I am thinking. Lev. We could publish your memoirs.* Talking-it-out." Was he still there? She gave him her best insight: "*Lev: you are putting yourself in the Isolator now. Now, your apartment is equal to your Isolator. Hello, hello? I criticize so you will improve.*"

"I've already left the Party." He meant she sounded like someone at an expulsion hearing. He hung up.

Ignoring the handkerchief's intimations of danger in "*bohemian, tubercular downtown,*" she drove to Augustine Manor. To forestall its further haranguing, she tucked five dollars under the head of a man sleeping outside the convenience store before entering the lobby.

No answer. A man in a wheelchair tapped on the glass of the residents' lounge. "Miss Patrice?" he said.

Stalina shook her head. Still no answer. She would just keep ringing. She would not let this insult stand.

Katya's name wasn't listed on any of the buzzers. "*The eye sees, but the tooth cannot reach,*" said the handkerchief and even though she knew it would find a way to follow, she threw it behind her as she closed the lobby door.

Yana

Hi, hi,

Yes, a lot of bombs went off, but only two people died, so the chances of anything happening to me or Pratik are minuscule. In the U.S., about 114 people die in car accidents every day, so.

Awakened Muslim Masses is only targeting Bangladeshis who've converted to other religions, Communists, Jatra dance fans, and certain lawyers. So we're fine.

What many people abroad don't realize is, the Awakened people are inept. Their bombs don't explode, or if they do explode, they injure a lot more people than they kill. 500 bombs and 2 deaths. Pratik says hi.

Yana

Milla

"*Eh, devka,*" Milla's mother said, handing her the tray and squeezing her shoulder-padded frame onto the side of the bed.

Milla began as usual. "Malcolm didn't just leave me, but also, he wasn't really there when we were married either."

"Physically present, emotionally absent," Stalina said, with the same relish she brought to reciting Russian translations of Shakespeare.

"Physically absent, too, though."

"Very bad."

"You know," Milla said, sinking back into her pillow. "I had other opportunities."

"Of course. All my girls have the best legs, small ankles from me and long from Papa." Stalina petted Milla's unshaven calf.

Milla took another bite of cinnamon cereal and started up again, reciting a fragment of an Anna Akhmatova poem, guaranteed to make her weep: "*This woman is sick / this woman is alone,*" but found she couldn't go into the next part. It would have felt ridiculous. "You can go to work now, if you want."

Her mother stared.

Milla shrugged. She was experiencing a feeling which it seemed almost too much trouble to identify. "I might be bored." When she had said the same as a child, her mother had not been very happy to hear it. ("*Maybe if we had a Blockade, you wouldn't be burdened with this terrible ennui?*") Now, however, Stalina wiggled Milla's earlobe and smiled like a mime.

Nadia Kalman

Katya

Katya, long-time family loony-tunes, family weakling, the sickly baby, that same one, was re-tiling the kitchen floor. If they could see her now — but her father didn't want to see her now. Not being the weakling meant not thinking about that.

"Bad-ass," Chino said from his bed, where he was writing a birthday card for his aunt in prison.

Old linoleum: a yellowing checkerboard. New linoleum: green frogs on a shining white background. She would make sure it stayed that way. She would make everyone go without shoes. "You know I'm just renting this place, though, right?" Chino said.

She nodded and opened the adhesive.

Chino covered his nose. Apparently, you were supposed to wear a mask, so she tied one of Roman's undershirts over her face. Chino turned his hooded sweatshirt around.

The first five squares were perfect, flush with her chalk line. She didn't mind, for once, Chino's bragging about his five thousand dollar signing bonus, his oft-revealed revelation that he'd always felt like an army of one. She hummed to herself. The frogs reminded her of Amston Lake — maybe she and Roman could go there, once she started working.

The door slammed open. Katya said, "Your money or your life."

"Jacked my shirt." She untied it and tried to hand it to him, but his boots stepped past, over the floor she'd cleaned and sanded.

"Hey." Her voice sounded young and surprised — not the kind of voice to make anyone stop.

He poured himself a glass of water and turned around in his own dark footprint. "Sorry."

"It's okay." She had a small advantage now. "Listen, like when I first moved back to Stamford, my parents did this like cold-turkey thing with me." He didn't look that angry. "Maybe you want to...it would be one thing if the K helped you, like, lighten —"

"*Don't nanny me.*" He opened the refrigerator and took out a head of cabbage, tore off a leaf and chewed.

Katya leaned her hand on the floor. She couldn't believe Roman wasn't affected by the fumes, or maybe he was, and that was why he was saying those things.

Chino put on his sunglasses. "Later."

"Pick me up something?" Roman said, but Katya shook her head so angrily that Chino closed the door without answering.

Roman tore off another leaf. "So I am one who needs to lighten, you think."

She pressed another tile down. She'd gotten them out of order, and a frog was missing half its face.

"But Katya is perfect shorty, right?"

"Look, you're the one who practically made me pee in a cup before our first date and now —"

In a deep voice, he said. "*I'm Brezhnev and comrades, I must say this chickie is crazy to think she can order around a man like Roman Pitursky.*"

Another square. You have to know what your energy is about.

"*Doesn't she know that everybody laughs at her cretinsky speech? Doesn't she know how lucky she is to have a normal man?*"

You have to —

"You fuck up floor," Roman said in English.

"I should just talk like you, right, my G?" Katya said, swaying to a standing position. Why couldn't they go outside? "The guys on your site never laughed at you? I saw them laughing." A mistake, if she ever wanted him to go back to work, but he wouldn't, anyway.

Roman pulled the brush out of her hand, reared back — would he hit her? "*She's just a sterva yobanaya, see?*" He threw the brush in the sink.

Katya didn't know what his words meant, but she knew what would happen next: how she would leave now, without packing, or finishing the tiles; how her mother would look behind her for Roman, and let her in; how her father would make a joke about the fall of the Roman Empire, and apologize; how Milla would

Nadia Kalman

try to explain something about marriage, and cry; how Roman would show up, drunk, fancying himself a Mayakovsky, only to be captured by the Neighborhood Watchers in their orange vests; how she would watch him through the window and would not jump out.

Milla

Milla stood outside Katya's door with a cup of valerian tea. "Kat?" The door was closed and music was blasting, just like when her sister had been a teenager. After a while, she and Yana hadn't bothered to try Katya's door anymore. No wonder Katya had run from a house where her own sisters had better things to do than to knock and wait.

Milla said, "I've got drug tea." She heard nothing in reply except a singer who wished he were a lamp. "I should never make a joke, ever. It's not really drug tea, just *valiryanka*, like Baba Byata takes when she visits."

Katya opened the door, looking as pale as she had at Milla's wedding. Milla held out the mug, spilling tea on her hand in her eagerness.

"Do you see this window?" Katya said.

Oh, no. She would have to get their mother involved. "I do see it. This window is actually real," Milla said. "What else do you see?" She hoped, for poor Kat's sake, that at least she was hallucinating elves or talking flowers, and not blood-filled gasoline pumps, as in a television film about a drug-addled single mother she'd seen recently.

"What kind of asshole hung this?" Katya pointed at the window's frame. "What kind of fucking retard doesn't level?"

"I don't know…what *kind*…" Milla put the tea on Katya's desk.

"Do you want to know how crappy this frame is?"

In the weeks that followed, the house became increasingly noisy. Sometimes, Katya asked whether the noise was bothering Izzy, but most of the time, she didn't. She never asked whether it was bothering Milla, Stalina or Osip; perhaps she imagined they felt grateful at the reminder of her ongoing fixes to what, to them, seemed unbroken. On weekends, Osip was driven before the force of Katya's improving will, looking back over his shoulder, with confusion and longing, at the television. On weekdays, Milla tried to assist her, but Katya could be very snappish. Sometimes, Milla wanted to say, "I have a child, you know," or, "I'm going through a divorce, you know."

One day, while Katya was at Home Depot and her parents were at the Chaikins', Milla called Theandra Carlisle and invited her out for a quick coffee, and offered to drive into Park Slope to meet her.

Roman

Roman opened the door. The television screamed, "My baby needs milk —"

"Cartoons," Roman said, but Chino shook his head.

An old man, bleeding, unbandaged, clothes torn, stood in a line in the sun. Behind him, a woman waved a bruised arm from her wheelchair. Roman's mother could have helped them. She tied her arm, nurselike, unafraid, her needle shone.

"I'm a U.S. citizen," said a woman in her underpants on the side of the road. Someone else in a wheelchair, head covered with a flannel shirt, brown-blue feet in plastic sandals. A stadium without water, shit on the floor, locked in, not even the babies allowed to cross the road to Wal-Mart.

"Shut up," Chino said.

A helicopter approached two boys and an old woman sitting on a roof. It poked its nose at them like a dragonfly. The boys got up and waved, but the woman knew better. The helicopter flew off.

Chino said, "You want some stuff, I know you steal it anyway. Here, just shut up." Water, gelatin.

A roof with an American flag, an inscription: "The water is rising please."

"I'm telling you," Chino said. The camera pulled back from the roof, back, back, and the people disappeared, and the roof, and all the roofs, disappeared into gray and black. Chino pushed him out the door, so he could disappear, too, to the house of the Molochniks, where all his problems had begun.

Buses swept exhaust back and forth before the library, and he gave the bus driver eleven dollars and a bonanza of change and the driver yelled because he didn't understand.

No one was home, the key was in the mezuzah: signs that he was doing what was right.

Upstairs, he took off his socks, stood in the bath, opened the faucet. Then he remembered the Molochniks' vodka and got out, splashing the tiles with his bare feet. He dried the floor with a bit of toilet paper: she'd never be able to say he never cleaned up.

He hefted the bottle upstairs and emptied the last of Chino's K crystals into it. Chino would understand. Roman had never liked the taste of vodka, but had been able to conceal this fact, and now would carry it to his grave.

He folded his Masta Killa tee shirt. Maybe Izzy would want it when he grew up. He put his underwear in the trash (and here he heard himself speaking, as if to an audience, voice reverberating, "*A man should not leave his dirty underwear behind.*")

He found Louisiana at the bottom of the geographical shower curtain and touched his finger to the green finger of land that poked from it. If only he could help. He wished them all well. What a thing: to lie down in water. Water made a bed for you, water received you when no one else would. The drain tried to take all the water but there was too much.

He held the vodka above his head and poured it into his mouth, gangster style. After a while, his mother's body floated towards him, bloated, scarred. Roman covered himself and shifted his legs to make room.

Osip

In the car going home from the supermarket, Osip and Katya listened to people asking for water on the radio. It felt strange to be driving in a car filled with food.

The telephone rang. "*Yanushka*," Osip said. "*Nu, how are you?*"

But Yana wanted to speak in English, her language of argument, about New Orleans. "This is your Bush," she said as he steered one-handed.

"Bush didn't build —" he had to switch to Russian — "*the levees, that's engineers.*"

"Tell me one difference between the Bush administration and the Pakistani army." The Pakistani army? Osip ran a red light, cars honked, Yana said, "Are you in your car? Drive to D.C. and protest." She finally said goodbye; she had other people she had to call.

"You should have just hung up," Katya said. He wondered about her: how easily, once she'd decided a person was not worthwhile, she carried out that decision. Even in her leaving Roman, which had been, without question, the right choice, Osip had been surprised by her lack of hesitation, how she'd mailed back the CDs Roman sent without bothering to listen even once.

They parked and Katya started for the house, carrying six bags of groceries. "Hey," he said, squeezing her arm, "who has the muscles?" She would go into the house and unload like a robot, take exactly ten minutes for lunch, and return to caulking the downstairs bathroom. Periodically, she would walk through the kitchen, and he would feel her eyes as he tried to relax with the paper, and then they would caulk together through the afternoon.

It was dark inside, so Stalina had not yet returned from Lord & Taylor, which had been her second home since Katya began her improvements. It sounded like she'd left the radio on — soft static. He flipped the light switch, but it only flickered, and above it, the ceiling sagged, dripped steadily from many small points, the way he had thought a rain cloud worked when he was little. "Katya —" he turned to tell her to get out of the house, but she was already running upstairs.

He dropped his bags and followed, feet sinking into the swamp of the carpet. Water pulsed from the bottom of the bathroom door. "Locked," Katya said.

Osip pushed her behind him, shouldered the door once, twice — metal crashed against tile, the shower curtain collapsed — a scream. Katya? She jumped past, clutched the shower curtain; no, something inside the curtain.

"Sorry," a voice said, from beneath Alaska. Osip waded a step closer. It was Roman, yellow as a supermarket chicken, in churning pink water.

***

"It looks okay," Stalina said a few hours later, uncertainly fingering the handle of her white paper shopping bag. She began to pick her way across the lawn. The neighbors were looking. Luckily, she didn't seem to notice. She'd left the car door open.

Osip tried to think of something authoritative and reassuring to say, called after her, "Little to no exterior damage."

"Half an hour," a fireman said at the door.

Damp, trampled envelopes were scattered like leaves in the front hallway. The mailman had come to their house as if it were any other, as if they would continue to order cable and pajamas — one of the letters had Russian curlicued handwriting, and a return address from *Novoe Russkaya Slovo* — someone else remembered his parents, perhaps correctly this time — but Stalina was muttering in the kitchen, and he stuffed the mail in his pockets and ran to her.

She was shaking a dripping lamb leg over the sink. "We have to cook this up right now, just get me a —" He threw it in the trash, steered her towards the stairs. "Always rushing me, *dyurgoet menya, my mother's rugs* —" She stopped at the door of their bedroom. Osip had carried Roman in there, put him on the bed as they waited for the ambulance.

"*Come.*" He pulled her into Yana's room, which was almost all right, and sat her on the edge of the bed.

He filled a suitcase with Stalina's clothing, putting the most cheerful colors on top — a sweater with a peacock, orange stretch pants — and went back downstairs to get her figurines. Only the leaping couple above the fireplace had broken beneath the weight of a chunk of ceiling plaster. When he came to tell her the good news, Stalina was kneeling on the floor of their room, going through the bedside table. She sprang up with two dark spots on her pantyhosed knees, threw open their dresser drawers and pulled out the remaining sweaters, nightgowns, socks, bras, piling them on the carpet, heedless of the damp. When she'd emptied all the drawers, she began pulling them from the bureau, upturning and shaking them. *"Rot and die, then,"* she finally said.

"Are you talking to me?" Osip tried to make a joke out of it. She let him bundle her out the door.

Roman

Katya knocked on the open door of his hospital room.

They were lucky: his roommate, a spry old man with a spider bite, slept inside his curtains. Now Roman could tell her everything he'd been thinking. But his mind caught on her, just her, her straight brows, her scratched hands. She'd been working without gloves again.

She said, "You don't look too great. But, you should see our house." A tiny smile: a joke. He laughed. It hurt.

He tried to sit up. "It was my bad, it was all my bad. Forgive, please —"

"Hey —"

Tears shot from his eyes. "I'm the *sterva yobanaya*, not you."

She rubbed her arms. He wished he had a jacket to give her. "Do you feel bad at all?" she said.

"Hell to yes, I feel bad, I —"

"About the house." She turned away, breathing hard. "That was supposed to be my parents' last house. Did you have even one thought about the drywall? The shelving? My mom's swan curtains, we made fun of them, but they were custom —"

Roman shook his head. "To keep it real: no. But now —"

"We'll have to break out the ceiling."

"I will fix —"

"You. Are you HVAC certified? As if. There's mold, which we can't afford, because the insurance doesn't feel like paying, because, according to the insurance guy, you're still in our family. Aren't we so lucky? I feel like such a retard for screaming when we saw you. After a second, it was totally obvious you weren't dead."

No one could ever want to kill himself after hearing that scream.

"*Kotletka,* listen —"

"No, you listen. You listen." He sat up in the posture of a perfect student. She slammed the door.

Lev

Leaf Day Morning. Osip's car turned into the manor's parking lot, skirting a glaring puddle. Osip came out and walked to the front. Osip came back. Osip and Katya came out, came back. Osip, Stalina, Milla, Izzy, Katya and Yana came out and disappeared under the lip of the roof. Osip's head emerged at the top of the ladder.

Of course they found me, he said. Did I imagine that my neighbors, and even Katya, once, hadn't seen me sneaking up here? If we left now, he said, we would still reach the rabbi in time for the ceremony. Didn't I want to honor our parents? Didn't I understand? Had I made myself into a complete defective? It was very hot. His head became reflective and he shielded himself with his hand. His mate and progeny came, one by one, or by two, and gathered themselves to him.

"*He won't come,*" Osya said.

"*Then let's go, Izzinka's getting dusty,*" Stalina said.

"*You won't come, the least you can do is give your speech now,*" he said. "*Do our parents mean anything to you at all? Aren't you proud of them?*"

All I could think of was an old children's song. It had been Milla's favorite when they first immigrated.

> "*Mama flies a great big plane, that is very good*
> *Mama makes a fruit compote, that is also good!*"

His wife held him back from me, "*Osya, you see how old he is.*" He commanded his family and they disappeared down and away.

Yana

Yana sliced into her steak. They didn't have steak like this in Bangladesh. Or, they had it, imported, for five hundred dollars, and people displayed it in their living rooms when you came over. Unfair, unfair. That was what Pratik called her. He hadn't been angry. In fact, he had been trying to show her she shouldn't be so angry "all the time." Electricity went out and there was nothing to be done about it. Try to relax, try to walk with all the others in large circles in the grassy lot. And in fact, the times he'd gotten her outside on outage nights, she had liked the peace, the coconut trees and the cows, how it was too hot for good clothes and how teenagers, on those nights, were allowed to flirt.

Her mother was questioning Milla about her new friend Theandra. *"Do you go out together and meet men? It's easy for women together to fall into a pattern of just sitting at home and complaining."*

Katya ducked her head in a smile — what was so funny? When she raised it again, though, she had the same clenched expression she'd worn for most of Yana's visit. A man — a boy, really, but still — had tried to kill himself over her. It was awful, it had wrecked their house, but if Yana had been Katya, she would have felt flattered. Sick. She took Katya's cold hand. "You know it wasn't your fault, right?" she said in an undertone.

Katya blinked and said, "Why would you even think — I wasn't even there," making Stalina halt mid-interrogation, and turn, and say, *"Of course not, Katyenok. What kind of crazy person would think that?"* Why wasn't Stalina asking Yana anything? She was the one who'd been away. Would it cost too much to call Pratik on the hotel phone?

Stalina

After dinner with the girls in the hotel restaurant, Stalina released them back to their room so they could gossip about men. Hadn't she always wanted them to be friends? Every time they laughed at something Stalina didn't understand, it was a victory of motherhood. The handkerchief would have asked why the girls hadn't *"comforted their destitute matriarch,"* so it was lucky Stalina hadn't been able to find it earlier. It would probably follow in a day or two. It couldn't have drowned.

Stalina's room was so quiet, she felt as though her ears were filled with cotton. She almost couldn't believe that she had ever had a house, and in it a collection of figurines, flocks of worries. She tried to make a list of what was lost. She tried to open a window. The Swiss bank building glimmered at her through the glass.

She turned on the television. The citizens of New Orleans begged for buses, trailed her through the channels. Why show these scenes, if there was nothing she could do? She called the Red Cross number on the screen and donated, but it wouldn't be in time. She threw the polyester blanket off her legs. She turned the television off, then back on again. Why hadn't they left before the storm? There was always a way, legal or illegal, if you really wanted to go —

Some time later, she realized she was lying in a ridiculous position, curled like a hedgehog, ruining her skirt. At least she had remembered to be silent. Her girls, in the room next door, couldn't have heard.

By the time Osip returned from his meeting with the insurance agent, she was in her nightgown, brewing tea in the coffeemaker. He was sweating, his shirt was unbuttoned, the tie with the ducks she'd bought him spilled from his pocket, he looked like a cabdriver, he refused tea, he vibrated beside her in the bed until she closed her Ulitskaya novel and said, *"Nu? He told you something new?"*

"We'll have enough."

"*Enough for what?*"

He spoke so quickly, it took her a second to recognize the language as English. "Enough for most happy plan for my Stalinatchka."

"Me?" She waved her hand. "I have no problem. *We have never been materialistic people. What, I'm going to cry over my curtains? Over the rugs from Azerbaijan, where the people hate us now? This was not the Point of Immigration. We can live in an apartment, we —*"

He grabbed her by the shoulders. "*Will go to Boston.*"

She pulled back. "*What's this nonsense now?*"

"'*Oh, my mother's in Boston, taking the wrong vitamins! Oh, Edward and his big, big lab in Boston!*'" Osip said in a high voice.

"*But you wouldn't even let me —*"

Osip rolled on top of her and patted a breast. "He is no match for my awesome love powers."

She squeezed a corner of the blanket in her fist. "Your job? You are now hippie?"

"Yes. I am hippie. I take early retirement. I will golf." He talked and talked, periodically rising for bouts of exuberant open-door urination. Didn't Stalina know that Milla's company had a branch in Boston? Izzy would meet so many children of the intelligentsia. Katyenok would come, of course; she loved the sea. He spread his arms across the pillows and smiled.

Nadia Kalman

7

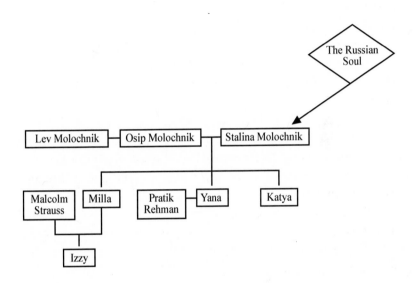

Leonid

Leonid Chaikin was not in the mood for this errand, and yet, here he was, activating his security system. He'd spent the day being trained not to act the way every single guy at his firm acted, all because some new hire — a secretary, at that — had ratted him out to HR. HR. What bullshit. He slammed the door. He should have bought a Mercedes, or even a Hummer; Porsches were too fragile. Some kids on bikes slowed to look at him and his car. He straightened, put on his jacket. You had to be a role model, no matter what was happening in your work slash personal life. He wished he'd brought a scarf. Damp brown leaves clung to his shoes.

Would there be a permanent mark on his record or not? Would the firm still send him to Switzerland? All he'd done was try to get a little something something going with Fiona. He hadn't even yelled at her yet, and it was a hostile environment? He sneezed into his hand, and for a moment had a pleasant memory of lying in bed, drinking hot milk with honey, his mother reading to him from Iacocca's autobiography. You couldn't call in sick for a sexual harassment workshop, or you'd have to start all over again. Nor could you get out of an errand, not when you were Leonid, and your mother had asked you.

His mother had actually said, *"It's what Russians do."* Excuse Leonid, but hadn't they emigrated to get away from Russians? Who but his mother had forbidden them to speak Russian in the house? Who had forced him through Little League, karate, ballroom dance, and yoga? She had raised him to be transnational, the General Electric of men (they needed him for Switzerland), and now, she didn't like it?

No one answered the Molochniks' door, so after a moment, he opened it. The living room was empty but for two orange folding chairs, and the floor was covered in some kind of plastic. He heard a man singing in Russian and followed the voice to the kitchen, where

Katya Molochnik was standing on a ladder, doing something to the ceiling with a tool he didn't recognize. He grabbed the front of the ladder. "You shouldn't be —"

"Oh no, it's safe," she said. Even dirty and shabbily dressed, needing only a few others to form a huddled mass, she was not bad looking.

"So my mom sent me to check up on you," he said.

"I'm okay." She tucked a strand of hair behind her ear. Was she flirting? He could use a consolation fuck. Did girls like her get pedicures?

"Mind?" He poured himself some water from a plastic jug. "You're really supposed to be using a paintbrush for that. Just saying." He raised his hands.

"That's after the plaster layer."

"If you say so." He smiled and shook his head. "What're you listening to?" It sounded like one of those old guys his parents sometimes put on.

"Galich." She sang along with a verse. *"What is a soul? Last year's snow."*

"That's pretty hard-ass," he said.

"Well, it's the devil talking."

"No, I like it." He swigged the water and tasted plaster.

"How about you?" She pointed at his headphones, which he'd forgotten he was wearing.

"Floyd, *The Wall*," he said, unlooping the headphones from his ears.

"I like that movie. Or I did in high school, anyway."

"Yeah?" Throughout today's workshop, he'd been thinking about the part where the giant, open flower swallowed the small, pointy-petaled one. He'd felt like the small, pointy-petaled one. "The parents are liking Boston, so I hear. How's the rest of the fam?"

She brushed some hair back from her eyes, streaking it with white. Even when she got old, she'd still look good. "Yana's back in Chittagong. Milla's in Provincetown this week, with Izz and Theandra."

"Thea —?"

"Her girlfriend. Theandra." Katya narrowed her eyes, but he wasn't about to say anything "inappropriate." Why was he constantly under suspicion? All he'd been about to say was that he wasn't surprised.

He said, "My mom wanted me to ask about Roman, too. She couldn't have him back in the house, after…" he gestured towards the upstairs bathroom, "so we don't know if he's okay, or…"

"Roma," she called. He was there? And being addressed in the diminutive?

Roman limped into the room. "Returning to the scene of the crime?" Leonid said.

Roman laughed in that immigrant way that showed he didn't understand, and said, "How's it hanging?"

Leonid replied in the usual manner. Katya hadn't divorced Roman? Roman was squatting in the house he'd wrecked? Seriously?

"Check it." Roman pulled a CD, jewel case and all, from the droopy back pocket of his jeans. "Romin Tha White Russian" was brandishing a hammer at a Winnebago in what looked like a used-car lot. "Money goes to New Orleans, for houses not trailers," Roman said.

"All the vast amounts of money you're making on this?" CDs were obsolete, hadn't anyone told them that?

"He's sold over forty already," Katya said, with a challenge in the movement of her chin.

"More like my friend Chino has sold, in Iraq." Roman put a hand on Leonid's shoulder. "But how I am thinking is, we don't need to live like Mafia to party like porn stars."

"Huh." They were far from partying like porn stars, from what Leonid could see. If Katya really wanted to party like a porn star, he could show her: amazing steaks, front-row Counting Crows seats. But that didn't seem in the cards. The plaster dust was making his cold worse. He wiped his nose with the back of his hand.

Roman said, "Like now, I have dance party, Westhill High. Bro, want to bounce together?"

Leonid shook his head, smiling. "Work tomorrow. I've got to be a good boy." How competitive could you get with a greenhorn cousin who misunderstood your insults and called you bro? And who was Leonid, if not a firm believer in family values?

Katya jumped off the ladder. "It looks good, right?"

Leonid sneezed, nodded.

Katya linked an arm through Roman's. *"Here is the path upon which hundreds of millions of people have already followed, and upon which all of humanity is fated to tread,"* she said in a strangely mannish voice.

Roman was laughing before she'd even finished. "Most dope."

Leonid held up an arm and staggered into the living room under the weight of an impending sneeze. It bellowed out of him, and his eyes ached, and his fingers — oh, God — were now webbed with mucus. He'd left his tissue pack in the car. "Are you okay?" Katya called. He had to get out of this house.

Leonid had a strange sense of being watched, from above, by some benign but not at all disinterested party, not God, definitely not his Grandfather Mendel, who'd called him a "soft boy" and died before Leonid got into Harvard, which would have shown him.

— A white handkerchief floated before his eyes, and fluttered, with a strange sideways motion, into his open hand. *"Batyushka, moy spacitel,"* my lord, my savior, emanated from parts unknown.

Nadia Kalman

8

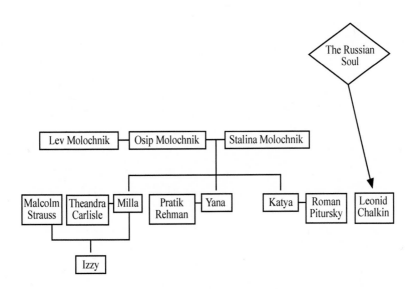

The end

Nadia Kalman

Acknowledgements

With many thanks to the following people, magazines and residencies:

Aharon Levy
Amanda Rea
Anne Kadet
Barbara Jacomba
David Leavitt and *Subtropics*
Deborah Schupack
Elena, Lev and Mikhail Kalman
Iffat Islam
I-Park
Jeff Parker, Michael Iossel and Summer Literary Seminars
Joe Taylor, Tricia Taylor, and Connie James of Livingston Press
John Crowley
Jonathan Dee
Josip Novakovich
Kathryn Davis
Lazar (of blessed memory) and Rachel Chalik
Alma Cales-Colon, Ernest Logan, and NYC CSA
Melissa Range
Pilar Gómez-Ibáñez
Rachel Monahan
Robert Stone
Roger Skillings
Salvatore Scibona
Sam Lipsyte
The 'Fords
The Antigonish Review
The Bards
The Crab Creek Review
The Fine Arts Work Center in Provincetown
The Gettysburg Review
The Levys and Levy-Maizies
The Madison Review
The Ragdale Colony
The Teachers & Writers Collaborative
The Walrus
The Wendy Weil Agency
Victor LaValle

Photo: Kambui Olujimi

As a child, Nadia Kalman emigrated with her family from the former Soviet Union, and grew up in Stamford, Connecticut, a town locally famous for once having had the second-largest mall in the country. Her short stories have appeared in publications both large and small, but mostly small. She now lives in Brooklyn, with her soul, more or less.